# THE <sup>MIS</sup>UNDERSTANDING BETWEEN US

# The ~~Mis~~understanding Between Us

Nishant Jha

# CONTETS

# **PROLOGUE**

He was sitting on the bench at the corner of the park with a flower in his hand, thinking about her. He was completely lost in her thoughts, when he noticed a girl in white top and a blue jean entering the park from the back entrance. He was not able to recognize the face as she was somehow far from him, she was looking here and there seeking for someone in the park when she noticed him and started moving toward him, as she was moving close to him, he slowly recognized her, it was she, her love of life, about whom he was thinking of, she came and sat beside her, took the flower from his hand and held his hands, and kept her head on his shoulder, he looked in her eyes and lost himself in the deep ocean, she slowly shifted toward him and sat in his lap, both of them could feel each other's breathe, they were completely lost in each other, he held her from her waist and hugged her tight, his heart was so heavy that tears rolled down his cheeks and fell on her shoulder she also wrapped her arms around him and hugged him back with the same intensity, they didn't wanted anything to come between them, they were so close to each other that their heartbeat could be felt by them and even the air could not make its way between them..

"Dhruv, let's go yaar," came Apurva yelling at Dhruv who was sitting in a corner in his room, lost in Nidhi's thought, Dhruv came out of her thoughts and gained consciousness. It was Apurva's birthday that day and she had booked a café for the celebration, all the friends had reached the café and were waiting for Apurva and Dhruv to come.

Apurva was Dhruv's best friend and knew how much he loved Nidhi and how alone he felt since the Nidhi was not with her, she wanted Dhruv to come with her and enjoy the party but Dhruv was not ready to go as he didn't had the courage to face her friends as they were all there when Nidhi accused him of not understanding her, not giving time to her, not letting her live independently, not making her feel loved, and what not, he thought everyone believed that it was Dhruv because of whom the relationship got spoiled, Apurva tried to explain him that no one thinks that he was wrong and everyone knows the things didn't worked out and it wasn't anyone's fault In that. After much efforts Dhruv got ready to go with her but on a condition that he will not get indulged much with the others and was just going because of her.

They reached the café where all others were waiting for them, she first cut the cake and them all others started celebrating and dancing on the beats, Apurva sensed that Dhruv was not comfortable their and was also feeling ignorant among them, she forced Dhruv to accompany her on the dance floor, Dhruv first resisted but after sometime joined her, Dhruv slowly came out of his thought and started enjoying the celebration.

They had their lunch there and then returned back, Apurva accompanied Dhruv back to his home and sat with him for some time, Dhruv held Apurva's hand and thanked her for being with him in his odds and downs, whenever he felt low he found her by his side, Apurva met Dhruv only a  few months ago but in a very short time she had become so close to him that they knew each and everything about each other, they both were of same thought that it is not about how long you have been with someone but how strong the bond between the person is, they both shared common interest, in a very short span of time they had become so close that they can understand each other's mood just by seeing the face.

Apurva tried making Dhruv comfortable and asked him not to think much about those things which hurts him, she made Dhruv gain some confidence that everything will be alright in a while just have faith in god and not to worry about the things that happened in the past. Dhruv cried his heart out with Apurva and felt somehow light and relaxed after that.

Dhruv thanked her again for being there with him at that time because he badly needed to talk to someone,

"oh, come on yaar it's not that only I remain with you in your downs but you also show up whenever I need you"

"But I genuinely want to thank you as I was thinking not to tell you anything today as it was your birthday and I didn't want to spoil your day with my negative thoughts,"

"oh, now you'll spoil my mood also, so you have separated me from yourself"

"I didn't mean that, don't misunderstand me"

Then conversation led to a humorous argument and after some time Apurva left for her home, and the day went by……..

# CHAPTER:- 1
# THE NEW BEGINNING

"Hey Dhruv come-on yaar we got to enjoy, we are in college now, we have not come here just to observe a girl dude." I asked him to come out of the class in the lecture break and come to the canteen to have something to eat. It was our first day in college and we were very excited for our college life to begin as we have heard much about college life from our seniors and elder siblings. Dhruv and I were friends since class tenth and it's been around three years that I've been enjoying life with him, Dhruv was a well-built tall boy, with enthusiasm and excitement filled in him, he used to remain ready to do anything for fun and making others happy, condition that it does not effects the ethics and discipline anyhow, I used to call him Mumma's boy as he used follow each and every instruction given by his mom even in her absence, he was a modest person and very soft spoken and a soft hearted person, he didn't mind if he does anything to make somehow happy which may even hurt him, he always tried to be the reason behind someone's smile.

We have decided in our class 12th itself that we'll take admission in the same college and spend atleast three more years together, he managed to take admission in maharaja Agrasen college in the first cutoff itself but I didn't met the cutoff till the third cutoff, he scored better than me, it was the time for the fourth cutoff and probably the last cutoff for me as after that the seats might get full for the courses we had opted for ourselves, we almost lost hopes that we will be together, but destiny had planned something else for us, when the fourth cutoff released I immediately downloaded it and looked for the cutoff marks of our course, yes, I screamed loudly out of joy, yes I had met the cutoff requirement and we will be together for another three years, I took admissions and eagerly waited for the college to start on 21$^{st}$ July.

And yes, today was the D-day it was 21$^{st}$ July today. We had downloaded our time table from the college website a day before the college, we had our class at 8:30 on the first day, so we decided to leave the at 7am on the following day as he did not wanted to get late on the first day and first class itself neither do I wanted to. I reached his home at exact 7 and called him to come, his mother came along with him and asked me to take care of him, we both laughed and Dhruv told his mom not to worry as we had seen the route and will reach safely. He was a pampered child and haven't gone anywhere alone till date which made his mom anxious, she asked, "jyada hanso mat tum dono, araam se jaana aur araam se aana, aur pohonch kar phone kar dena." His mother handed him the lunch box and asked us to feed ourselves when we feel hungry, she had put 2 extra chapatis for me too.

Dhruv wore a blue jeans topped with a white shirt which suited his fairly white face, he added a black moccasin shoes to complement the blue white combination, the small Nike bag on his shoulder completed his dashing guy look for the first day in college, on the other hand I had put a cargo jeans with a red T-shirt on which I had put a check shirt to give it a three piece look, I had completed my look with a blue campus casual sport shoes which I specially bought for the first day of our college, I had two thick notebooks in my hand which I put in his bag and I walked barehandedly, he wanted to handover his bag to me as I had made it heavier by putting my notebooks in it but he didn't gave me as it would distort his look, we touched his mother's feet and took her blessing for our first day, and then left for college.

We reached college at 8:15 and the college entrance was not yet open, we sat on the boundary walls on the periphery of the college walls, Dhruv took out his phone and called his mom and informed her that we reached safely and well before time, we started discussing about what we will do in the break between our lectures as we had a lecture from 8:30-10:30 and then other at11:30-12:30, we had a free hour between the lectures, we were sitting and discussing when a tall girl in white top and blue jeans having sharp features, glowing skin, deep sparkling eyes, butter smooth lips, slim physique, and an attractive pinkish red cheeks came and sat on the wall parallel to the one on which we were sitting, she had a small teddy shaped bag with her, Dhruv got mesmerized by her eyes and went on staring her since the time she came there, I asked Dhruv to come as the gate has opened and we needed to go for the class, but I doubt if he listened to me or not, he didn't got up till the time that girl got up and entered the college, we walked toward the gate and Dhruv came back and started talking to me, he said, "she is so beautiful na, I hope she is in our class only, come fast let's see where she goes" when we entered the college we seeked for her but we could not find her anywhere, then we headed toward the college admin area and looked for the time table there on the notice board and our class room number, it was room number 112, we asked the guard bhaiya for the way to room number 112, he guided us toward the 1st floor and told us the way toward our class room, we followed his instruction and reached room 112 which was in one corner of the building, and as soon as we entered the room, to our surprise we found the same girl sitting on the second bench of the third row which left Dhruv dumbstruck and he jumped out of happiness but controlled himself as he didn't wanted to be observed at first, he contained his happiness and walked into the classroom and sat on the third bench of the second row so that he can see her but she cannot. I sat with him on the same bench he was continuously staring at her and I was waiting for the professor to come, meanwhile many other student came, we interacted with some boys and in the first meet itself we somehow formed a group, Dhruv had a magnetic personality he joked and talked In such a manner that everyone became his friend in just a small chat, after a few minutes the professor came and introduced himself to the class, and asked everyone to call out there name at their place only in order starting from the first bench of the first row, everybody called out there name in order, but Dhruv ignored everyone and was just waiting for the her turn to come, passing from us her turn came and she stood on her place and introduced herself, "myself Nidhi Singh", Dhruv reiterated her name in his mind which eventually came out of his mouth but it was so slow that only I could hear this, I asked him to please focus on what the professor was telling us, but he was busy reading her face, soon the professor started teaching us but Dhruv was busy observing her with utmost attention like she is the syllabus which he needed to study in the college and had joined to take a degree in that girl, the professor completed his lecture and left after which we had an hour before the next lecture starts, "Hey Dhruv come-on yaar we got to enjoy, we are in college now, we have not come here just to observe a girl dude." I asked him for the fifth time, but he resisted for the fifth time, I was feeling hungry and did not wanted to waste even a single minute of our first day in college, " so stubborn you are you don't care about your friend" I was saying these words when I saw he stood up and asked me, " yaar tu kab se baitha bola jaa rha hai, chal bahar chale, kahin ghum k aate hai." I noticed that Nidhi also stood up and was leaving with two other girls, we both got up and left the classroom and went in other direction so that she doesn't think that we are following her which eventually we were doing. We were having an eye on her and were noticing where she was going, as soon as she vanished our sight Dhruv hurried toward the canteen, he had seen Nidhi going that way, Nidhi entered the canteen from the gate which opened inside the college but we entered the canteen from the entrance which was on the ground side and behaved like we are unaware that she was also there. We saw her sitting on the corner chair in the canteen and looked for a vacant chair which we didn't found, I noticed that there were two chairs vacant on the same table on which Nidhi was sitting, I suggested Dhruv to lets go and sit there it was an opportunity for us to talk to her and become friends, but he was so nervous that he didn't agreed to go in front of her, I somehow managed to convince him to come with me, we approached that table and this time I had to take the initiative which I have never done in the past three years when I was with him, I went on the table and introduced myself, " hey, I am Vipul, can we sit here with you guys as there are no other vacant chairs in the canteen," Nidhi nodded and spoke in a soft tone, "yeah sure", she was having her lunch, I asked Dhruv to please take out our lunch also, as I had not bought any lunch with me, Dhruv took out the lunch and we started eating.

I haven't seen Dhruv so much anxious about anything in the past three years, he has fallen for a girl just in the first sight, he was a strong believer of the fact that love cannot happen in the first sight but he himself had experienced the same, Dhruv was a kind of extrovert and didn't hesitated in speaking to anyone whether he knows the person or not, but today he was not able to grasp some strength and talk to a girl.

Dhruv somehow managed to gather some strength and stretched his hands toward her, "hey I am Dhruv Sharma" this sentence acted as an icebreaker between them, after which Dhruv started his butter and sugar coated talks, which made Nidhi feel comfortable with him, they had a nice conversation, he was continuously looking into her eyes, and got mesmerized by her voice, it was 11:25 till then and we headed toward the class together, we reached our class and sat on our seats where we were sitting in the first lecture, soon the professor came and started teaching us, and Dhruv started telling me about Nidhi as if I was not there when they were talking, the professor noticed us talking and scolded us in her first class itself, Nidhi had a smile on her face seeing us getting scolded, we apologized for our deeds and promised the professor that we won't repeat the mistake. The whole class was making fun of us, but Nidhi didn't do the same instead she signaled us to stay quiet and not to bother ourselves with all these and just focus on the lesson.

As soon as the class ended and the teacher left the classroom Nidhi stood up and took his bag and started leaving the class when Dhruv called her from behind, and asked if she was leaving for home or will she come back in the class, Nidhi told us that she will be leaving for home soon after exploring the college a little, Dhruv asked her if she doesn't mind if we accompany her in exploring, Nidhi nodded her head in agreement and we three left the class together and headed toward the ground, we sat there for some time and shared our experience of getting into the college, about our schools, our home and many other things, meanwhile we exchanged our contact number and Dhruv looked at it as an achievement. We found out that Nidhi's stop falls in our way itself and we decided to leave for home together.

We left the college and saw an ice-cream stall in front of the gate, it was a hot sunny day and the sun was scorching high above our head, Nidhi asked if we'll have ice-cream and we nodded, Nidhi took three cornetto and Dhruv paid for it, I was getting a treat in between the two, we sat on the walls where we were sitting in the morning and had our ice-cream, after finishing we left for the bus stop which was just a walking distance away from our college, there was a temple on the road on which we were walking, Dhruv when passing from the front of the temple closed his eyes and wished for something in his mind, we reached the bus stop and waited for the bus, when the bus arrived we three boarded the same bus and started talking about the experience of the first day in college, Nidhi told it was a good day and praised the teachers knowledge and way of teaching which Dhruv had not noticed as he was busy noticing her, I shared my experience and till the time Dhruv could have said anything Nidhi's stop came and she bid a bye to us, soon we also reached our home, the first day for which we were so excited came to an end but a new chapter had started in the life of Dhruv and Nidhi. A happy start and a healthy start, which no one knew will change their lives to a great extent.

Nishant Jha

# CHAPTER: -2
# THE FIRST CHAPTER

Dhruv was continuously thinking of Nidhi since he came back from college, he was thinking to text her on WhatsApp, but a flood of thoughts stroke his head every time he picked up his phone to text her, what will she think of me, am I a despo?, is it ok to text her?, we haven't been friends for long then why am I texting her?, and many other questions arose in his mind, after having dinner with his father Dhruv sat back in his room and finally sent "hi", overcoming all his thoughts and questions, and the text had a single tick in front of it and the time read, 22:13, he then eagerly waited for the tick to become double and blue and get a reply from her, but to his disappointment, the tick didn't changed by 00:05 then he decided to go to sleep, but his sleep was taken away by a girl who was not replying his message, he was tossing and turning in his bed unable to sleep, he again and again picked up his phone and switched on his wi-fi and checked if he got a reply, he opened his phone for the 14th time when the message was read and he got a reply, "hey Dhruv" his eyes sparkled seeing her message, he got excited again,

"where were you? I was waiting for your text for the past two ours"

"oh, sorry I was busy with some stuff, by the way why were you waiting for my text?"

"no nothing as such, just wanted to have some chat with you"

"Ok, so what do you want to have a chat about?"

"oh yes I was asking if you'll be coming to college tomorrow", Dhruv somehow tried to settle the blunder that he has created with his text in excitement

"Yeah, I'll come, are you coming?"

"yes, I am also coming"

"ok so let's meet in the morning, got to go and sleep, good night"

"good night, see you tomorrow"

Dhruv kept his phone aside and started waiting eagerly for the morning to come, he started thinking about her, what will I say to her when I'll meet her tomorrow? how will I talk to her? Will I be able to talk to her or not? How will she react? Firstly I'll try to make a conversation with her and make her comfortable with me then I'll try to spend time with her and talk for hours, I'll ask her likes and dislikes so that I don't do anything which she don't like, I'll try to mold myself the way she likes, I'll joke in front of her and try to make her smile, haan this will be okay, I should text Vipul and tell him to get ready early tomorrow we'll reach college before her, "hey Vipul, are you awake?" he texted me, but I had fallen asleep much before this text and so I didn't replied, he saw that the message was not delivered so he made a call to me, I didn't realized the phone ringing for the first two times but the third call woke me up and I saw Dhruv's name flashing on my screen, I picked up the phone,

"kya Hua bhai, soya ni tu abhi tak" I said on picking the phone

"dude I can't fall asleep, the thoughts of Nidhi are running in my mind and those thoughts are not letting me sleep" he replied

"oh Romeo, you can do this Aashiqui tomorrow also, just go to sleep and let me sleep to, otherwise we spend the day like a zombie due to lack of sleep, so better go to sleep and don't act like a hardcore Majnu" I replied

"ok dude I'll try to sleep, tu soja, by the way I had called you to get ready early tomorrow morning, we have to reach before her" he said

"ok dude, let me sleep now, if I'll sleep now then only, I'll be able to wake up early and get ready early for college" I said and hung up the phone

Dhruv resumed his thoughts about her and fantasizing his life with her and fell asleep somewhere midway.

The next morning, he woke up very early and dressed up like a true gentle man, he spent more time in front of the mirror today than ever before trying to look as perfect as he can to impress Nidhi with her looks but Nidhi was not that kind of a girl who gives any attention to looks but it was Dhruv's duty to try everything to impress her, he put on white shirt and a blue denim so that his bright fair face can get high lightened and he looks more attractive, he finally got ready and called me to come fast, this was the first time that he got ready before me to go somewhere, I quickly got ready and reached his home, I greeted his mom and dad and asked Dhruv to come Dhruv came out and touched his mom's feet before leaving,

"aunty ji, bless him for victory, he needs your blessing" I said trying to tease Dhruv

"kyu bhai? On which mission are you on that you need blessings for victory" his mom asked

"nothing mom, he has gone mad" Dhruv tried to cover up

"aunty ji, it's a secret mission, you just bless him, don't you want him to win" I said to his mom

"vijayi bhava" his mom blessed him, I laughed on this and then we left for college.

"Vipul bhai, have you gone mad? You would have put me in trouble" Dhruv asked me
"what did I do?" I asked her
"dude, mom would doubt me now" he said
"are don't worry, you got your mom's blessing you will surely win" I said
"what" he amazed
"what, what?" I teased him
"what will I win, am I contesting something?" he said
"you'll win what you want to, her heart" I said and laughed
"Vipul bhai don't do this yaar, I don't know if she'll even accept my friendship or not, and you are behaving like she is waiting for me only and she is already my girlfriend" he said
"ok, leave all this, ask her when will she reach college" I asked him to text her, he too out his phone and texted Nidhi,
"Good morning", she was online and replied as soon as the message got delivered as if she was also waiting for his message,
"we are reaching college in the next half an hour; how long will it take you to come?"
Her home was not too far from college and it took her merely 20 minutes to reach
"it'll take me 20-25 minute to leave now, wait for me before going to class" she replied,

Her message brought a wide smile on his face, we reached college and sat on the same spot we were sitting the previous day and waited for her to come. He was so restless waiting for her that every now and then he went to check out the lane if she was there or not and finally, she came we got up and went in the class together, the professor had not come by then, I and Dhruv sat on one bench and Nidhi in front of us, we were talking to each other when we made a few more friends, Nidhi introduced us to Megha and Muskan with whom she was sitting in the canteen, and we introduced them to Nikhil and Sohail, it was 9:15am and the professor has not come till then, we sent Nikhil to enquire about the professor in the staff room, the professor told Nikhil that he will not take the class today and asked him to kindly write the attendance on a paper and hand it over to him, Nikhil noted down the names of all the students and gave it to the professor, we all decided to go to ground and sit there till the next class, Nikhil and I went to play badminton where megha and muskan joined us and Sohail went to meet his other friends in the other department, now Nidhi and Dhruv were left alone, Dhruv took the opportunity and took Nidhi with her to the food point where they sat and talked much about their likes, dislike, choice, goals, past and many other things, this conversation was the one which made Nidhi and Dhruv close to each other. They sat there for more than an hour didn't give any attention to the time.

I called Dhruv and asked him to come back to the class, as the next class was about to start, they came together, I was sitting with Nikhil, megha and Muskan where they joined us and sat together on the same bench, it was the starting of a new relationship between the two which was more than just friends, we took the classes and left for home, we all were together but Dhruv and Nidhi were having their time together, they were walking a few steps ahead of us, we boarded the bus and Nidhi and Dhruv were continuously talking, Nidhi deboarded the bus at her stop after which they started talking on WhatsApp, we reached home and Dhruv didn't spoke a single word to me the entire way and remained indulged with his phone talking to her, he just bid a bye to me when I was leaving for my home. He was completely lost in Nidhi and talking to her.

Days passed by and they became a bit closer to each other with each passing day, they talked late till night and proved that late night conversations are the best to make bond with someone, they shared each and everything about them to each other in the late night chats, about their past experiences, their secrets, their strength, their weakness and everything, they knew everything about each other by this time, the rumour about their relationship floated in the class by then but they called each other just friends, I was his best friend and he never lied to me, so, on one day when we were working on an assignment at his home I asked him directly,  if they are in a relationship,

Dhruv said, "yaar, you know na I fell for him on the first day, I saw her, I don't know if she likes me or not, we have become good friends but I haven't expressed my feelings to her yet, I fear if she would accept my proposal or not, and it may affect our friendship also."

I understood his concern and told him that he should at least confess his feelings to her, she'll surely accept his proposal, as anyone can easily identify that she also liked Dhruv as she carry a different type of glow and smile when she is with him, she used to remain happy when with him, I told him that she might be waiting for him to confess his feeling I told him that I had asked Nidhi about her feelings for him one day when he has not come to college and Nidhi was restless and was not able to focus on studies as she was continuously texting him, she had told me that Dhruv had become a part of her life and she has started feeling differently for him, she said she don't know if the feeling is love or something else but she feels differently for him, which she said was an unknown feeling for her as she had not felt like this ever before for anyone else, this brought a wide smile on Dhruv's face and I somehow convinced him to express his feeling to her, and after knowing this he also agreed to express his feeling on 17<sup>th</sup>of August, which was Nidhi's birthday, he decided to take a cake for her and express his feelings after celebrating her birthday.

Dhruv took a promise from me that I won't tell about this plan to Nidhi and will keep this as a surprise for her and also help Dhruv in planning everything for the same. I promised him and then We continued with our assignment and Dhruv started planning her birthday in his head.

# CHAPTER:- 3
## SURPRISE

"Hey dude, lets meet at the Vasundhara enclave market, at the food point on the right side of the plaza, bring Nikhil, Sohail, Muskan, and Megha with you and take care that Nidhi should not get an idea about what we have planned for her", I called Vipul as I was making some arrangements for celebrating the birthday of my beloved Nidhi there, I had ordered a heart shaped cake on the bakery and had brought a large teddy bear packed in the wrapping paper for her, I had also booked the cafe at the top floor of the plaza and asked the restaurant manager to please decorate the restaurant with red heart shaped balloons and arrange some soothing music for us, I had also bought a ring for her, which was not in the plan and no one except Vipul knew that I was going to propose Nidhi.

I was nervous and excited at the same point that I am going to propose my girl and I'll be giving a new name to our relationship between us, which was called "yeh Rishta kya kehlaata hai?" by all our friends, I was preparing myself with the words and the feelings that I'll speak to Nidhi when I'll propose her, even I was making notes on my hand that what all I need to speak so that nothing goes against my feelings, it was more than 2 months that I was looking for an opportunity to tell my feelings to her and it was today that I got a chance to do so, I wanted to utilize the opportunity in the best possible manner. I was lost in my thoughts standing at the gift shop when Vipul came with all the friends, I was getting the teddy bear packed at the gift shop I asked Nikhil to bring the teddy bear to the café and hand it over to the boy in the café meanwhile I went to the bakery with Vipul to take the delivery of the ordered cake, the shopkeeper made us have a look on the cake which was exactly what I wanted, perfectly shaped, red in color and the name Nidhi written on it with white cream, the cherry on the top was completing the cake, we took the cake and went to the café and handed the cake to the boy at reception and asked him to bring it when we ask him to, I checked for the decoration and all other things which I had planned in my head since the day Vipul provoked me and I decided to propose her on her birthday. When I was completely satisfied, I asked Muskan to call Nidhi and ask her to come to the café, Nidhi was closest to muskan after me, Muskan called her and she said she'll be there in a few minutes, she was not coming to college that day but was just coming for us as we have requested her to come for an hour.

I was continuously looking the road from the window to check if she had come or not, anyone could've identified the nervousness on my face but none of my friends said anything to me, I saw a metallic silver color Maruti Suzuki ciaz stopped at the entrance of the plaza, Nidhi also had the same car so I checked for the number plate, yes, it was her car, she had arrived, I sat back and asked Muskan and Megha to go down and bring her up. Muskan and Megha left to bring her up.

My heart had started beating at a higher pace than usual, I was being more nervous with each step she was taking toward the café, again a flood of thoughts stroke my mind, but Vipul understood the dilemma of  my thoughts and confronted me to be calm, she is not going to bite you or something, just relax, I kept an eye on the door and each passing second at that moment felt like a millennial, time was crawling and the wait was not going to be over soon, with each passing second my heart was increasing the pace, I was curiously waiting for my princess to step in, and finally the door opened Muskan and Megha entered first, and yes there was my princess, Nidhi had arrived in the café,

I raised my head above to look her and as soon as I saw her, my heart skipped a beat, the time stopped in her eyes, the cold breeze started flowing, the sun became brighter than usual, and all the planets seemed to have arrived themselves in a single line..

She was wearing a white one piece dress, with a white high heeled flat shoes, her hair opened with a white hairband on her head, she was looking like an angel which the god had sent from heaven just for me, just to light up my life, and fill happiness and love all over, I somehow managed to stand straight and not the expression on my face express the feelings on my heart, I welcomed her, Nidhi was also surprised by seeing the decoration in the café, she asked me if it was for her, I nodded my head into a yes and made her sit on the chair comfortably and sat beside her, Nikhil teased her and asked for party and Sohail accompanied him, Nidhi smiled and said dude "dude jo order karna hai kar lo, mai iske liye hi to aayi hu aaj". I signaled the boy at the reception to bring the cake for us, he hurriedly sent a boy with the cake and the boy served the cake to Nidhi "for you ma'am" Nidhi got surprised by the cake and asked for who had bought it, everyone signaled toward me, I said, "leave it ki kaun laaya, let's cut the cake" she smiled and asked for the knife, the boy handed her the plastic knife and put candles on the cake, Nidhi blew the candle and the café echoed the sound of melodies of happy birthday, the boy played a birthday song in the music system, which added a little to the surprises for Nidhi, as soon as she cut the cake, the balloons busted and sprinkled sparkles on her, which made my Nidhi looked cuter than ever before, she took a piece of cake and made me eat first and then to all others, we all took some cake and handed the rest to the café boy and asked him to distribute among themselves, Nidhi asked if it's over or something else was left for her surprise, she didn't knew the biggest surprise was still not unveiled, she went to the washroom to wash her face and hands which we spoiled by applying cake all over her face, I asked the café boy to play the music for us, by the time she returned I was on the floor in front of the music system to dance, Nidhi came and sat on her chair, I asked her to join me on the floor, she denied, but when I forced her she came and joined me with muskan and megha, I took it as an opportunity, held her hand and kneeled on my knees,

"life has taken an entirely different turn since the day I met you, I fell for you on the first day when I saw you sitting outside the college, my heart started beating for you only, when we talked on the first day, your voice mesmerized me, and I was completely into you, when we became good friends, I lost my heart to you, I smiled because of you, I remained cheerful thinking about you, I have never thought of anyone since the day I met you, you are the first thought in my mind when I wake up and last thought in the night when I go to sleep, you made my college life worth spending, the day you held my hand while crossing the road, I felt like never leaving it, I like my name when you call me, I like my hand when you hold it, I like my eyes when you look In it, I love myself when you are with me, you came into my life like a sunshine and brightened up my life with the grace you possess, I want to be with you forever and want to gift myself to you,"

I expressed my feelings for her in the best possible manner I could have done, I took out the ring from my pocket and opened it in front of her,

"I know I am bad at expressing my feelings, but I love you from the bottom of my heart and really want to spend each and every second ahead with you only. Would you except this gift in your life"?

I waited for her to forward her hand toward me, she gave me her hand and I put the ring her ring finger, she pulled me up and hugged me tight, she started crying on my shoulder,

"stupid I was waiting for this day since a long time, you took so long to express your feelings and made me wait for such a long time, I haven't received a better gift than you ever on any of my birthday, I love you idiot" "just promise me that you won't leave me ever In any scenario, whatever may the situation be, you'll always be by my side and we will tackle the situation together"

"I promise"

Everyone except Vipul was shocked and surprised by everything that they just saw, they knew us but they hadn't expected that to happen at that point at that instant, Vipul clapped and broke the silence in the café, he was happy for me, he came forward and hugged me and congratulated me,

"see you were unnecessarily worried and nervous about expressing your feelings, I knew that she likes you and will definitely accept your proposal" said Vipul

"what! Was he nervous about it?" asked Nidhi

"yaar you needed not to say this in front of everyone" I told Vipul and everyone laughed,

"should we congratulate you for your birthday or for this new relationship" teased Muskan

"arre we have to congratulate her for the relationship, she will get many wishes for her birthday but only we can congratulate for her relationship" added Megha

"as you wish" said Nidhi

"dude if you all are done with this prem prasang then we should order something to eat, I am feeling hungry" said Sohail

We ordered the food for them and ate together, when we were done with the food, I settled the bill and sat there for some more time, we all were talking and enjoying the time when Nidhi's phone rang, it was her brother calling her to come back home,

Nidhi asked us to let's go now as she had told her brother that she'll return in an hour and it was more than two hours that she was with us, we were about to leave when I stopped them,

"now is anything else left" asked Nidhi,

"the last thing I promise" I said, and signaled the café boy to bring the teddy that I have kept for her,

the boy arrived with the packed teddy bear seeing which a wide smile captured her face as she liked teddy bear very much,

I took the teddy bear from the boy and handed it over to her "a teddy for my teddy" I said,

On which everyone gave me a sarcastic smile and then laughed together,

She took the teddy and we left for home,

She dropped me and Vipul to the bus stop and left for home,

"I love you" I whispered in her ear while leaving the car,

"I love you too" she whispered back
We smiled and soon she faded from our site,
The most awaited moment of my life came to
an end and I was the happiest person on earth
that day.

# CHAPTER:- 4
# TEACHER BY HEART

Dhruv was very happy after the day he proposed Nidhi and she said a yes to her, Dhruv was so much into her that he was not able to focus on the studies and he feared that he may not be able to pass the semester exam, he was sitting on the corner bench in room 112 when Nidhi noticed her worried face and came to him said, "you seem to be somehow worried, is everything ok?" Dhruv nodded his head and said, "yeah, I am completely fine, why would I be worried" Dhruv did not wanted Nidhi to feel like he is holding her responsible for the lack of focus on his studies which eventually will hurt Nidhi but Nidhi knew Dhruv so closely that she can tell his mood just by seeing the way he breathes. Nidhi left at that point but signaled me to meet her in the corridor, I asked Dhruv to stay their while I am coming in a few minutes from the washroom, I came outside the class and found Nidhi standing there waiting for me,

"what's wrong with him? He is not talking to me properly since a few days, whenever I ask him, he always says everything is ok but I know he is worried about something, something is bothering him" said Nidhi

"Nothing, he is just worried about his studies, he has been a meritorious student in the school and had scored good marks always, his mother believes him to be good in studies which he actually is, but in this semester he was not able to study and he fears that he might fail the exam which will disappoint his mother which he never wants" I explained her,

"and why he hasn't focused on his studies this semester?" asked Nidhi

"he was so into you that he spent much of his time talking to you or thinking about you,"

I explained Nidhi in the simplest way the reason behind Dhruv's worried face but this explanation provoked a thought in Nidhi's mind that I was blaming her for Dhruv's inefficiency in the studies which I never meant.

Nidhi kept that thought aside and went to Dhruv and asked her if it was the reason behind his worried face,

"ji baby I was not able to give proper time and focus on my studies this semester, the syllabus is almost completed and the exams are approaching and I could not understand a single topic from our syllabus" said Dhruv

"bas itni si baat, and you are worried like you have lost all hopes in your life, don't worry Dhruv, we'll stay back in the class for an hour or more after all the lectures get over and I'll teach you in that time, we'll work together toward our studies and get good marks,"

Dhruv smiled and gave a thank you look to Nidhi

"Now don't carry this look on your face as you don't look good this way" said Nidhi in light mood,

The professor entered the class and Nidhi went to her bench and sat with Muskan there, I and Dhruv sat there on the last bench itself,

Dhruv paid complete attention in this lecture as he gained some confidence and thought that at least he should study the remaining topic in the lectures and the left out will be covered by Nidhi,

The lecture ended and we did not had any more classes that day, everyone left the class but I and Dhruv stayed back in the class, Nidhi saw us and she stayed back too, she called us to the front seat to teach, we jumped to the front seat and faced backward where Nidhi was sitting, Nidhi took out his notebook and pen and asked Dhruv to pay attention,

"which topic do you want me to teach you?" asked Nidhi

"anything that you feel can be easily understood" said Dhruv

Nidhi started teaching her and Dhruv paid his utmost attention toward her as she was the only person Dhruv paid attention to, Nidhi took 45 minutes to complete a topic and made

Dhruv to do some questions so that she gets an assurance that he understood what she taught, Dhruv completed the questions with ease which made him more confident, Nidhi asked let's leave now but Dhruv was not ready as he wanted to spend some more time with her and asked just 15 minutes more, Nidhi was not in a mood to stay more but Dhruv somehow convinced her, Dhruv jumped to the second bench and said, " mam can I sit with you?"

"yeah, sure my child" said Nidhi

And they both laughed, Dhruv took her hands in his and sat quietly thinking something,

"now what are you thinking" asked Nidhi

"why do you love me so much?" said Dhruv

"because you love me this much" answered Nidhi

Dhruv's heart was overflowing with the love that Nidhi gave him, Dhruv looked into her eyes and his heart sank into her deep eyes, he was not able to speak a single word after that, Nidhi hugged him and said,

" I am angry at you, you were not telling me your worries, baby we are together not just for sharing each other's happiness but also the worries, the pain, the challenges, the odds, the sorrows and each and everything that we have with us, you know I always had a void in my heart since the time I lost my dad 10 years ago and no happiness around me was able to fill that void, I always tried to get indulged in other activities and forget his memories but he never faded from my heart and I always used to think about him whenever I sat alone but since the time I met and you and you became a part of my life I never felt that emptiness in my life, I started being happy internally and never wanted to look back you had filled that void in my life, I was always incomplete but the day you proposed me and hugged me I instantly felt that the void was filled I won't say you took his place in my heart but you never let me think of him, the way you care for me, the way you pamper me, the way you do things to make me smile and everything that you do for me, you never let me go to the past and think about him, you made me complete that day, I always share each and everything with you but today when I saw you worried and not telling me about the reason, I felt bad, please never do such thing in the future"

Tears rolled down his cheeks seeing Nidhi's love for him, and he felt bad for not sharing his worries with her, he did not want to hurt her but unknowingly he did,

"I am sorry for what I did in the past few days, I am sorry that I didn't talked to you properly, even I shouted at you, I lied to you, I ignored you and what not, sorry for all I did, I promise that I won't repeat this ever and always share each and everything with you, please forgive me this time," he held his ears and apologized for what he has done,

I noticed that Nidhi was an emotionally weak person and that Dhruv has become his weakness, she can tolerate and bear any pain in her life but even a small thing breaks Nidhi and she gets hurt by small things.

Dhruv was also not wrong on his stand that this may go against his relationship as he didn't wanted to blame Nidhi for his studies as he knew it has nothing to do with Nidhi but it was his mistake that he didn't balanced his love life and studies in a proper manner which adversely effected his studies.

But the thing which Dhruv feared the most had happened and the thought that Nidhi was affecting his studies had stroke Nidhi's mind, but Nidhi was not showing this on her face but had the thought deep inside her heart,

These classes after the classes with professor Nidhi continued till the college closed for preparatory leaves some days muskan also joined us to learn the topic from Nidhi meanwhile I Nikhil and Sohail used to roam here and there in the college premises sometimes we went to the gym sometimes in the ground to play cricket and joined them after Dhruv gave a call to us to leave for home, Nidhi completed the syllabus and prepared him for his exams that he gained some confidence and was sure that he'll pass the exam.

The college closed for preparatory leave and not much time was left for the exams, Dhruv had got the 10 years book photocopied which Nikhil bought from daryaganj and started preparing from that only, Dhruv and I used to study together and whenever we felt any difficulty in any question we used to discuss among ourselves and solve if we both were not able to solve that question than we took the a snap of the question and drop the question in the WhatsApp group in which only Nidhi, Muskan, Megha, Sohail, Nikhil, Dhruv and I were there, Nidhi was the first to reply with the solution of the questions that Dhruv dropped from his phone but somehow ignored or lately replied the questions asked by others This became a point on which all the others teased Nidhi and Dhruv, on which all laughed together,

Days passed by and exam day has come, we all met before the exams and discussed our last minute doubts and we all wished each other all the best for exam, and entered our respective classes, Nidhi and Dhruv sat in the same class and Nidhi helped him in completing the exams, Nidhi also showed her sheet to Dhruv whenever he got stuck in any question, this way Dhruv was able to complete his first exam, we had four subjects in our first semester and all the exams were completed in a span of 9 days.

It was our last exam the next day when Dhruv dropped a text in the group to ask all of us to stay back after the exam and enjoy the last day before the vacations together. We all agreed to him to stay back and assembled in front of the college gate, we decided to go to the food plaza first and eat something and decide the plan ahead, we sat on the corner table under the tree at food plaza, Nidhi and Dhruv sat together as usual I asked everyone about the order, Sohail and Nikhil wanted Singapore noodles and Megha  and muskan ordered a plate a chilly potato and Dhruv settled with Nidhi's choice, and they ordered a plate of tandoori momos and I decided to eat all from their plates and enjoy all which all of us did, placing the order separately was just a formality as we all shared all the things that came on our table, we sat there for half an hour or so talking to each other, teasing Nidhi and Dhruv and enjoying our food and after finishing we decided to go in the park on the back side of the food plaza but Muskan and Megha wanted to return to their pg as they wanted to do their packing and leave for home as soon as possible so we didn't forced them to stay back with us, Sohail and Nikhil accompanied them and left with them and only I Dhruv and Nidhi were left, I also wanted to leave but I couldn't as Dhruv wanted to spend some more time with Nidhi as after that they will not meet until the college reopens for the next semester, and if I left and Dhruv's mom sees me at home than it will create a huge kiosk so I had to stay back with them. Nidhi and Dhruv sat in front of each other in the ground holding hands in hands, I took out my phone and started playing games in it,

"how were your exams?" asked Nidhi

"all were good and I am sure that I'll score good and all credit goes to you" replied Dhruv

They continued with their talks for an hour and were not in a mood to go when a call from his mom interrupted their private space, she was worried as Dhruv hadn't been this much late to reach his home ever since he joined the college, she asked him to come back. Dhruv could not disobey his mother so she asked me to stop my game and leave for home, Nidhi bid a good bye to us and left we also came back.

Nidhi and Dhruv used to talk much in the starting of the vacation but gradually their long conversations became short,

"hey"

"hi"

"howz you"

"I am doing great, just missing you a bit"

"I am missing you too"

"tell something"

"nothing special, you tell"

"same this side"

"ohk then, will talk latter"

"yeah sure"

This was the only conversation which they did in the past few days, Dhruv always replied like he doesn't has anything to talk which annoyed Nidhi and made her feel disappointed, Nidhi was disappointed that the guy who used to talk so much that he never stopped even on asking him to stay quite is now short of talks and doesn't has anything to talk, the thought of being ignored and left out stroke the her mind.

Dhruv was enjoying his favorite show on YouTube when he saw a Whatsapp message notification from Nidhi, he immediately opened the message which read,

"baby I am going to my mama ji's place and hence won't be able to talk for some days now, please don't text me as, if anyone catches me talking to you there will be a huge kiosk in my life which I believe you also don't want to happen, take care"

Dhruv became a bit tensed by this message as there hadn't been a single day since they met each other that they hadn't talked, Nidhi had been to her mama ji's place in the mid-semester break also but at that time she didn't asked him not to talk, it was strange that the girl who took the promise of not leaving each other's hand in any scenario is asking not to talk, Dhruv became tense and recalled all the conversation in his head that he had with her in the past few days, is she annoyed by the way i talked?, is she not happy with me anymore?, had I done anything wrong?, and many more such thoughts flooded his mind,

"can't we talk for even an hour at any time in the day?" he replied

"no, I won't be able to, and if a get a chance to talk ill surely text you"

"ohk, take care"

There were eleven more days left for the college to reopen on 1st January and Dhruv couldn't talk to her so he was eagerly waiting for the college to reopen so that he can talk to her, Dhruv was also hopeful that she will text him in between and kept waiting for her text.

# CHAPTER:- 5
# THE DIARY

Dhruv started thinking of the past few days recalling each and every moment spent with Nidhi and also about the conversation he had with her, he was thinking that there must be something wrong or he might have done some mistakes because of which Nidhi was not talking to him, every now and then he picked his phone and checked if there was a message from Nidhi, if she had texted him to talk but every time he got disheartened she hadn't texted him, Dhruv was being helpless and very much sad as it was the first time that they had not talked to each other for 3 consecutive days. Although their conversations had become short since the past few days but short a conversation with her mattered a lot to him, he used to be cheerful and excited even by that short conversation, he wanted to talk to her so badly but was unable to. He decided to write a diary and talk to it about all the thoughts and feelings that he felt in her absence. He took out a new diary from his book shelf and took some color pen and started writing in it,

Friday, 22nd of December,2017

10:30pm

Dear diary,

This is dedicated to the one who unknowingly captured my heart so badly that it has become nearly impossible to spend a second without thinking of her. My heart reminds me of her with each and every beat, she has become an integral part of my life which can't be separated from me by any mean, she remains with me with every breath I take, with every blink of eye, with every heartbeat, with each and every drop of blood flowing through my vessels. She is with me in each moment of my life.

It's been a while that I had talked to her and every second these days passed like a millennial which was very tough to pass, I had never thought that these days will also come when I won't get to talk to her and I was not mentally prepared to face these days. I haven't felt this kind of loneliness in my entire life as I am feeling now when I am not able to talk to her. She had asked me that she'll text me whenever she gets a chance to and I am waiting for that only, hoping to get her text soon.

Saturday, 23$^{rd}$ of December,2017

6:35 pm

Dear diary,

It's the fourth day and I haven't received her text yet, the wait still continues, I am being very much restless and tensed as I am not getting to know even about her well-being, hoping for the best.

From today onwards I have decided to talk to you and tell you each and everything about what I feel for my love as she is not talking to me and I want someone to talk to as I am missing her badly and I don't have her to tell all this, I know I might be looking somehow selfish that I came to you only when she is not there and maybe I'll leave you when she starts talking to me again, but I can't help myself with this as she doesn't let's any other thought strike in my mind when she is there with me, I don't need anyone else when she is talking to me, so in the very beginning of our friendship I apologize to you for this kind of behavior.

Ok! So, let me tell you about her and how much she matters to me,

Nidhi is the bright light in my dark life, she is the support that anyone wishes for, she is happiness of my life, she is the reason I smile, she is the reason I enjoy, she is the one I look for in a crowd, she is the pole star in the night sky shining bright always, she is the boat in my drowning life, she is the shield protecting me from all negativities, she is joy whenever I feel sad, she is everything to me. Since the time I have her in my life it seems as life has taken an entirely different route in which joy, happiness, prosperity, love and peace has replaced the misery, sadness, hardship, hatred and agitations which were there in path before I met her, she has completed me in every way.

Today I was missing the day when I proposed her and she hugged me for the first time, this is the first time since than that we haven't talked to each other for such a long time, the day we hugged it felt like our souls have united and become one, she held me so close to her that the frequencies of our heartbeat matched with each other, that day was a turning point of our life when we left all the things in the past and decided to move ahead and create our future together. It was the best day of my life as I had proposed her which was the best thing I did in my life till now. I wanted to tell her how much I am missing her but she is not talking to me these days so I told you, thanks for listening to my thought and being such a good friend. I'll get back to you tomorrow till then Bubye.

Sunday,24th of december,2017,

11:30pm

Dear diary,

The fifth day also passed without getting a message from Nidhi, I kept on waiting for it restlessly, but its ok, she might be busy somewhere and might have not got any chance to text me, she'll surely text me once she gets free and get a chance to do so.

I waited for her text just like the day when I was waiting for her at EDM (East Delhi Mall) near Anand Vihar, it was our first date, I and Nidhi had planned to go for a movie that day, There was a new movie named A gentleman in the theaters that day, we chose the show of 11:00 am and decided to meet directly at the mall, I reached the place at 10:30 am and waited for her there only, she reached there at 10:50 am, my eyes glowed on having a sight of her. I stood up and waved my hand to signal her, she saw me and came running toward me, I opened up my arms and hugged her, she hugged me back and she apologized for being late and then we headed toward the theatre , I had already bought the tickets for us, A1 and A2, the seats we have decided to book for ourselves by seeing the seat arrangement online, it were the corner seats of the first row from the top, we entered hall no 2 and settled at our seats with the assistance of the boy standing at the entry, the movie was about to start but there was no-one except us in our row, a few people were sitting in the rows in front of us but none in our row, the movie started and Nidhi held my hand in hers and laid her head on my shoulder, I laid back towards her, i could feel her breathes on my arms, I wrapped her up in my arms and she felt comfortable as it was her safe place, Nidhi was watching the movie on the screen and I was watching the same in her eyes, I could not divert my focus from her for a second as we haven't got an opportunity till that day to spend some quality time with each other, we never had been left alone by our friends, one or the other always remained with us at any point of time, so I didn't wanted to lose this opportunity to dive in the deep ocean of my love's eyes, we were talking to each other when a romantic scene appeared on the screen, there was an awkward silence between us, Nidhi looked toward me and I bent forward we were in close proximity of each other, our breathes became heavy and our lips were inches apart from each other, she closed her eyes and our lips met, the time stopped for a second, my heartbeat became fast which could be easily felt, Nidhi held me by my face and I held her tight in my arms, it was our first kiss, and a passionate one, I bit her lower lip while she slid her tongue in my mouth and we had a strong tongue fight that day in which I won, we were lost in the kiss while she explored my body with her hands and I slid my hand into her top and reached out to her bra strap when she pushed me back and said, "not now, we are in the movie hall and not in our room" it was something which erected a milestone in the path of our relationship. The movie ended and we left from there taking a different aura and different feelings than what we used to be before the movie, we were happy with our togetherness, we than had some food in the food court on the top floor of the mall and then returned back our homes, a different kind of silence was prevailing between us after the movie till the time we left our homes, after which a text message from her broke the silence and we started talking normally after that.

That was how our first movie date was. With each and every passing moment and act we became more closer to each other. Ohk I need to sleep and dream of her as it is the only place where I am meeting and talking to her these days, Bubye...

Monday,25<sup>th</sup> of December 2017,

8:30pm

Dear diary,

The sixth also passed without getting a message or call from Nidhi, but it's okay, I am hopeful about getting a message from her tomorrow...

It was Christmas today and the Mausam is awesome, as there were a couple of episodes of rain showers since the morning and the air had become cooler, the breeze became soft and every time it stroked my face I felt Nidhi's touch on my face, this kind of weather reminds me of the day when it rained heavily and we enjoyed the rain together,

It was 17th of September and it was raining heavily since the last night the weather has become cold, the weather had not become clear in the morning also so my mom asked me to not go to college that day but Nidhi had asked me to come to college as she liked rain very much and wanted to enjoy the weather with me, so I asked my mom that I need to get some important work done from the college and I need to go at any cost. Mom was not ready to send me but I somehow managed to escape the situation and left for college, I called Vipul and asked if he'll be coming to college but he said no so I left for college alone, and reached college at 9. Nidhi hadn't reached college by then, I called her and got to know she'll be reaching in the next 5 minutes so I waited for her at the entrance only, I noticed that there were not many student in the college that day, many had not come due to the weather so the college was nearly empty that day with only a few hand-full of students out there.

Nidhi came in a the next few minutes as she told me and we entered the college together, first we went to our class to check out if the class was going on but found no-one there so we decided to go upstairs on the second floor and enjoy the view from there we reached upstairs and stood in the corridor in front of room no 215 from where nearly the whole garden area of the college was visible. The trees were extra green that day the grasses seemed to be very happy, the chiming sound of leaves striking each other seemed to be playing melodies for us the small flowers and plants looked like they are dancing,

"see the nature is celebrating our one-month anniversary in its own way" said Nidhi and held my hand, it gave me goosebumps and an entirely different feeling of togetherness and unitedness with her I held her other hand and pulled her toward me but she stepped back.

"we are in the open corridor my love and I don't want any kind of PDAs" she said

"ohk my love but there is no-one around," I replied

"that's why I am holding your hands" she said

After that we stayed there for a few minutes and decided to go to the ground and sit there in the lap of nature. We went and sat beside the basketball court in the ground where no-one in the ground can get a sight of us, and sat there.

I laid back in her lap and started talking to her, she started playing with my hair and we were completely lost in each other, an ocean of feelings flooded my heart, her lap felt like my safe place and I wanted to sleep there my entire life.

"give me your ear I want to tell you something" I said

"you can tell me normally also, no-one is listening here, just you and me" replied Nidhi

"Nature also has feelings what if the air listens and tells somebody in its path, I want it to be within us only" I said,

She bent downward toward me and asked me what do I wanted to tell, I held her face and gave a little peck on her cheeks, she blushed a little and then started beating me, "what was that, ye dhokha hai, I won't talk to you" she threatened me,

"ok fine, I won't do it again, but at least give me a reply of what I told you" I teased her

"bhaago yaha se" she said playfully

We were enjoying our best time there in the pleasant weather when the rain added a cherry on top of the cake and fulfilled the remaining. I stood up and started running to save myself from getting wet when Nidhi held my hand and stopped me,

"why are you running? Let's enjoy the rain" she said,

And we stood there in the rain throwing water on each and other enjoying the weather to the fullest. Nidhi was not ready to go until rain stopped completely. I asked her that we'll get sick if stay in wet clothes for long so let's go home quickly and change. She hugged me and then left for her home and I came back home.

It was one of the best days in my life till date.

Thursday, 28<sup>th</sup> of December,2017
9:25pm
Dear diary,
Pardon me that I didn't came to you in the past two days, I'll try to be regular from now on. The ninth day had passed and I still didn't get any message or call from her, I saw her online today on WhatsApp but she didn't texted me I felt hurt, I wanted to text her but I remembered her last message that she wants me to not send her a text till she texts me, so I didn't texted her and became offline, it wasn't the first time that we had not met for so long but it the first time that we hadn't talked for this much long. The previous experience of not meeting her for this long was during the mid-

semester break. She had left for her mama ji's home one week before the week long break started as she had some event at there, but we used to talk much during that time, I had also called her before the break ends and she had agreed to come, after coming back to her Home we decided to meet and go to Gurudwara Bangla Sahib.

I left from my home on my FZ at 9am and decided to pick her up from EDM mall, we had decided to meet there at 9:30am but I didn't reach there on time because of some traffic near the vivek vihar red light, when I reached she was already there waiting for me, I noticed her from a distance and stopped my bike in front of her, we bid each other a good morning, and she sat on my bike, I asked her if she sat comfortably and may I start the bike, I started moving when received her permission, firstly she sat maintaining a bit distance from me, but after a kilometer or two, she slowly slid forward and held me by my waist and put her head on my shoulder, making herself comfortable on my bike, I slowed down my bike and started moving slowly as I found the way to be far better than then the destination (safar khoobsurat hai manjil se bhi). When she moved her face on my shoulder it tickled me and  wave of some strange feeling ran down my spine, I removed my helmet and hanged it on the rear view mirror of the bike and started moving bareheaded as I liked her touch and wanted her to be more closer, we decided to park the bike at Patel chowk metro station and then go on foot from there, we reached the metro station within an hour and moved on foot from there, it was a bit more sunny than any other day during that time and I didn't had anything to cover my head, Nidhi took out her stole from her bag and put it on our heads, we moved under the same stole and reached Bangla sahib, we sat there in the main hall for quite some time, she sat there keeping her eyes closed and praying something, I looked at her face and felt like all my prayers and wishes had become meaningful that I got her in my life, we then came out when the sun became a bit mild, we also had lunch at the langar served there and then we sat by the Sarovar adjacent to the Gurdwara, our feet partly dipped in the water, we sat there for more than an hour enjoying each other's company, we just enjoyed being with each other without saying a single word, the sun set in front of us, the picturesque beauty of that place at that time looked like the heaven came down on earth just for us and the angel from heaven is sitting by my side holding my hand, when it was around 6 in the evening we decided to leave for home and left from there, we again walked till the metro stations having ice-cream on our way, I took out my bike and we came back, I dropped her at nearest point to her home and then left for my home,

"let me know when you reach home safely" she said,

"ohk, baby"

And the beautiful day ended here…

I didn't found one or two dates after this in his diary, Dhruv was so much lost in her thoughts that he forgot about each and everything and he didn't even came out of his room, when I entered his room I always found him sitting in that very corner where he had kept lord Ganesha's idol which Nidhi gifted him a few days before the exams, mentioning "always pray to god before leaving for any work, god ji will help you tackle all the problems in the path and complete the work efficiently". He always sat there only, praying to god that everything becomes normal soon between them. I used to spend some time with him and then leave after making him understand that she might be busy somewhere and soon call or text and nothing will go wrong, so no need to worry. But it seemed like I didn't succeed in my task and he is still not able to make his heart understand the fact that he is not talking to her since a few days.

He continued to write such instances in his diary till the time he met Nidhi again in the college and talked to her and after that as he wrote in his diary stopped writing.

# CHAPTER:- 6
# THE FIRST FIGHT

It was 1$^{st}$ of January and the college reopened that day, no-one was going to college that day as it was new year's day and everybody had some plan to celebrate their new year in their style, but on the other hand Dhruv didn't had any plan moreover he was very impatient and anxious about going to college, he wanted to go to college and meet Nidhi as soon as possible, he even asked me to come to college but I had other plans to celebrate my new year and I wanted Dhruv also to come along with me but he wanted to go to college so I said, "she will not be coming to college today, you also don't go"

"she'll come, just come with me, it's been a long time that we met, so she'll not wait for long to meet me now" he replied

"ok, just call her and ask, if she is coming to college or not"

"you know na she had asked me not to call her"

"so, let me call her and ask if she is coming or not"

"ok fine, call her and let me know" he said

I cut his call and called Nidhi, her phone was switched off, I tried a several time but all attempts in vain, I even sent a message to Nidhi on WhatsApp but the message did not get delivered and I didn't get any response from her side, soon I received a call from Dhruv,

"hello, what did she said?"

"her phone is switched off"

"so, come fast we'll go to college"

"ok fine, we'll go on my bike and see if she had come or not, if she will be there than I'll leave you there and come but if not then you have to come back with me. Fine?"

He agreed to my terms and soon I reached his home on my bike, I picked him up from his home and left for college, the whole way he was talking about her and what he'll be doing and saying on meeting her after so long, he seemed to be anxious, nervous, impatient all at one time, it looked like he is meeting her for the first time, as soon as we reached the college and I stopped he jumped off the bike and ran toward the college,

"park your bike and meet me in the classroom" he shouted

I parked my bike in front of the college gate as there were no other bikes parked there that day, and then I ran toward the class greeting the guard uncle a happy new year, and reached in the classroom to look for Dhruv where he was sitting alone and Nidhi was not there, Dhruv felt disappointed and all his feelings faded away in a fraction of second after not finding Nidhi there in the college,

"let's go to the ground, she might be sitting there with megha and muskan" I asked him to come to the ground, he had no other option other than listening to me and following my suggestions, he stood up and we went to the ground, we didn't found her there also, we then went to the canteen, and all the places where there was a possibility of Nidhi being present but to our disappointment we didn't found her anywhere in the college, I asked Dhruv if I should call her one more time, he nodded his head, I tried calling her but received the same response, her phone was still switched off,  I asked Dhruv to lets go to home and get ready for party but he wanted to wait for some time, I sat with him at the college entrance with him for an hour and then we left from there when Dhruv himself asked me to.

Dhruv didn't came for the party with me as his mood was spoiled. He was waiting for this day since the college closed and when this day came it brought disappointment for him, he spent his day in his home only, packed in his room...

I called Dhruv to ask him to come to party several times but he was not ready to come in any case, lastly on forcing him to come he agreed, he came to my terrace where I and few of our friends had arranged a DJ to dance and some other arrangements to enjoy new year eve, Dhruv came there and sat in a corner, everyone was shocked seeing Dhruv not dancing on the beat as he was the one till last year who grooved on the DJ beats since it started and till the time the last song was played, that Dhruv was sitting in one corner, everyone easily identified that there was something wrong with Dhruv he is worried about something, on asking he hid his feelings behind a wide smile on his face as he didn't wanted anyone to know about him, on request from all other Dhruv even came to dance but he did not stayed for long there, after a song or two he excused himself and left for his home, everyone noticed his water filled eyes and heavy heart that he wanted to hide.

Dhruv ran toward his home and directly went into his room picked up his diary and made the last diary entry in it,

Monday, 1st of January,2018

11:35pm

Dear diary,

Happy new year, The College reopened today and I wanted to meet Nidhi today, but she didn't came to college, Vipul even made some calls to her and even messaged her on

WhatsApp but she didn't gave a reply, her phone didn't connected the whole day, I want to talk to her and know about the reason why is she not talking to me?, why is she behaving like this?, I wanted to hug her badly, if she is angry at me, she should tell me na, I would've apologized to her, at least she should tell me na what's wrong between us, I can't handle this silence anymore I want to talk to her, I want to talk to her now, everyone is enjoying the new year today and I am sitting here, I also wanted to enjoy but not without her, all my celebrations are just myths if she is not with me in that, I missed the day of our freshers party sitting there with my friends seeing them dancing , when we enjoyed each and every moment with each other. I wanted to dance there but only with Nidhi like we danced in our freshers party, Nidhi was standing and clicking some pictures of hers when I pulled her hand to dance, she held my hand and I stopped in her eyes, she looked at me and I looked into her eyes, we were lost in each other, she put her other hand on my shoulder and I wrapped my other hand around her waist, our lips not ready to speak a single word, our breathes becoming heavy, heart beating faster than usual, we forgot that we were standing in the college ground and a crowd of students was surrounding us, we had nothing to do with the surrounding or even the song that was playing on the DJ, we were dancing on the beats that were playing in our heart and we didn't wanted to listen to outer environment, with each step we took we inched closer to each other, in a few minutes we came that much closer that we felt each other's breathe on our shoulder, it was when the professor took the mic on stage and announced that it was the last song to be played that evening that our concentration broke and we returned to the real world. It was the first day that we realized that we wanted to be in each other's arms till out last breathe, it was the day when I realized that I wanted to be in the shade of her hair lying in her lap. We had spent the best time together, we will spend the best time together but I don't know why there is a break in between that had separated us to an extent that we are not talking to each other, I want to meet her now only, I want to talk to her immediately, I don't know how but I want to talk to her...

He was looking very helpless in this entry I wished I could've done something and made him talk to her but I couldn't do. As soon as he completed writing this entry and put his diary aside his phone vibrated in his pocket, he took out the message in hope that it could be

Nidhi's message, the lock screen popped up the name of Nidhi, she had sent him a message, as if his heart's call reached hers and she didn't not wanted to see his Dhruv like that, Dhruv jumped out of happiness, tears rolled down his cheeks, finally he received a message from her, he opened her message in a hurry,

"Happy new year" her message read,

"Happy new year dearest, where are you?  I was waiting for your message since a long time, is everything all right?  have you come back from your mama ji's home?   Will you be coming college tomorrow? Didn't you miss me in these days? how did your days went?" Dhruv couldn't control his emotions and wrote all at once,

Nidhi wanted to tell him how much she missed him, how hard it was to pass these days without him, how long was she waiting to text him, how did she managed to hide her feelings from everyone, how badly she wanted to hug him when she cried and missed him, but remembering the way he had talked to her in the past few days and the blame that he put on her of being responsible for his lack in studies, she controlled her emotions and wrote, "I am fine and I'll come to college tomorrow, Bubye" Dhruv understood that something has hurt Nidhi so bad that she is not talking to her love without whom she didn't spend a single minute, the way Nidhi messaged confirmed that Nidhi is furious on him, but he was not getting what should he do now, how should he apologize and how should he relieve the resentment in his love's heart, he did not wanted to react at that time so he sent her a message, "why Bye?, we haven't talked for so long, aren't we talking now also?"

"will meet in college tomorrow" she replied

"ohkzzz, gunnie, tc, c u 2morrow" he sent her a message and she became offline after reading his message,

Dhruv called me after that and told me all that had happened with him at that point, and asked me for suggestions to tackle the situation and get his Nidhi back as she was, I didn't had anything to say on this matter so I said, "just keep calm, meet her tomorrow and clear out all the difference sitting together, you know she loves you more that you love her, so she'll not remain furious on you for so long and just figure out what had hurt her so bad and apologize for your mistake and everything will be fine," "for now just go to sleep, its 2 am now, good night dude" I hung up the phone saying this and slept but Dhruv was restless in his bed and couldn't sleep in spite of trying hard, the next day he got ready at around 7 am and called me to come fast, we didn't had our class at 8:30am that day but Dhruv couldn't wait more to meet Nidhi now, I said, Nidhi will also not come this early, so relax we'll leave for college at around 8:30am but he didn't wanted to wait and asked me if I was coming or not otherwise he'll leave alone, so I surrendered and went with him, we reached college by 8:30 and found Nidhi sitting in front of the main gate as if she was also waiting for him, she had never come so early in the entire semester, Dhruv couldn't contain his excitement on seeing her after so long time, he went and hugged her tight, unaware of the surrounding and the fact that there were not just they two there but other people also, soon Nidhi pushed him back and asked to go to the ground and sit there, it was evident from her eyes that she was not ok, and she was not the same Nidhi which she used to be, we went to the ground and sat on the bench under the trees on the basketball court side, Nidhi didn't spoke a word and sat there silently, Dhruv tried to build a conversation several times, but she didn't replied, I excused myself and left them alone so that they could figure out the differences and clear them out. As soon as I left the place and left them alone, Dhruv jumped off the bench and sat on the ground in front of Nidhi, "Dhruv

I don't want to create a scene here, please come up and sit on the bench" she said, "why my love what happened? Can't I sit here and stare you as it's been a while that I've seen this face" Dhruv tried to make the environment lighter but Nidhi was in no mood of doing so. "Nidhi I know that something is bothering you from within and it is related to me, atleast tell me, atleast talk to me, you know how badly I waited for this day, I wanted to talk to you so badly, i wanted to share each and everything I did in this vacation, I was waiting for your messages so badly, even I wrote a diary in which I wrote each and everything I missed about you in this days as I didn't had you to talk to, I missed you so badly love"

"oh please, stop all this, you are just saying that you wanted to talk but you never did when I messaged you, you always remained busy with Vipul or some other friends when I messaged you, whenever I asked you to talk, you never had anything to talk, and when I stopped talking you got many thing to share with me, where were these things when I tried messaging you and talking to you every now and then, I felt like I am being a chepster and you don't wanted to talk, I am unnecessarily trying to talk to you, I wanted to share my day with you but when I texted you, you always asked me to talk later and when I texted after some time you were so much exhausted that you didn't had that much energy that you can talk to me, oh please Dhruv, don't act like you cared too much, you never did, I stopped texting you just to give you time and space so that you couldn't blame me for not letting you enjoy your vacation as you did for your lack in studies, each and every day passed  like a millennial for me, I wanted to text you, but then I recalled you might not have anything to talk, you might be busy doing something, I wanted to meet you in between and go to some place with you like we went in our mid-sem breaks but you spoiled all, you knew that I had no-one except you to talk to, but still you didn't talked to me properly those days, what do you expect me to do in these situation." Nidhi burst and cried his heart out.

All the things flashed in front of Dhruv's eyes and all the time he didn't made a conversation with Nidhi, all the time he mentioned that he missed his classes to do something for Nidhi, all the incidences flashed in front of him, he sat speechless, he wanted to explain each and everything and tell her that he never blamed her for his studies rather it was his fault that he didn't managed his love life with his studies, he wanted to tell Nidhi that he wanted to talk to her but he literally had some work assigned by his mother which he couldn't have ignored, he wanted to tell that he wanted to talk to her all the time but due to some reason or other was not able to do so, but he did not wanted to hurt Nidhi more and just said,

"ohk fine, I except that these things came to your mind just because of what I had done, but it's not like what you are thinking of it, I accept my mistake and promise you that I won't repeat these things in future and won't hurt you ever, please forgive me this time"

Dhruv spoke softly, all the anger flowed down with tears from Nidhi's eyes and she cried on his shoulder badly.

"sorry my love, I know I had unknowingly hurt you badly, but please trust your Dhruv that I won't repeat this in future and will always keep you happy"

"promise me?" Nidhi spoke in a cute accent still crying

"I promise"

And they hugged each other and all the differences between them flowed in the stream of their love, I loved seeing them together, I texted Dhruv "are you done, should I come now?"

Dhruv showed this message to Nidhi and they both laughed and Nidhi made a call to me from her phone, "come on dude, you played a nice trick to leave us alone"

I went there and sat with them and shared some smiles with them, it seemed like they both had come more closer to each other after this incidence, after a few minutes Nidhi spoke out "I wanted to see the diary that you were saying you wrote these days" Dhruv was not ready to give the diary to her but after her cute requests he agreed and handed over the diary to her but on a condition that she won't read it there but at her home.

Nidhi turned a few pages from the back of the diary and read a quote written there,

"hum dono do dhaage hi to hai, humaare beech me jo Rishta hai vo hum do dhaago k beech ki knot, hum dono ko koi kitna bhi door karne ki koshish kare humaare beech ki knot or tight ho jaaegi na" she smiled at Dhruv and we left for the class…..

# CHAPTER:- 7
# DEPARTMENTAL FEST

Nidhi and Dhruv cleared out all there misunderstanding and differences by talking to each other and started spending their time with each other like they used to before all this kiosk in their life, they played with each other, they teased each other, they helped each other, they pampered each other, moreover they were least bothered about the surrounding world and were happy with each other's company till our departmental fest in which Nidhi was in the organizing committee and Dhruv was given the task of managing the sound and music system, as he was interested in music and had a technical mind so he knew about how to set up the sound system and all, our department had decided to host a certain event in the fest which included a debate competition, a quiz competition, some cultural things and the most interesting was the treasure hunt for which most of us were waiting.

The day started with the quiz competition at 9:30am in which Nidhi had participated and Dhruv and I were sitting in the last row as spectators. The teams were divided according to the rows, there were four rows and so were the teams, the quiz were categorized in 3 rounds, the first round eliminated one team, second round eliminated the second team and the third round was the decider which gave the winner, Nidhi's team reached the final round and Nidhi answered the final and decider question which made Dhruv jump out from his seat and shout Nidhi's name and cheering for her, some  eyes turned toward Dhruv in suspicion and I held Dhruv by his hand and made him sit back on the seat, after the quiz was over there was another quiz for the audience in which the person answering correctly was given a chocolate and Dhruv was the one to grab the maximum number of chocolate, he grabbed 6 chocolate out of the 10 given and he distributed those chocolates among the students sitting there and shared one with his love Nidhi celebrating their win, we left from the hall and started preparing for the next event which was debate, none of us participated in the event and just remained in the audience and managed the event, the third event was the talent showoff in which all the participant showed different talents like someone sang songs, some recited poetry written by them, some danced and some gave a mono act, the surprise of that event was Nidhi's performance about which none of us had an idea, Nidhi was about to give a dance performance, Nidhi came on the stage and tied a knot in her top to make the top a crop top, she danced on the song shape of you by ed Sheeran, her moves on the song were so smooth and graceful that none can move their eyes from her, one guy from the crowd commented on Nidhi and her physical beauty, he shouted "she is so smooth and soft that if she gives me a chance to spend some hours with her I'll make her a bit a hard" this comment from him triggered Dhruv and out of his reflexes he slapped him tight, this incidence created a great blunder there and made Dhruv victim of the incidence, Dhruv had to face the anger of the teachers and other organizing members and all held Dhruv responsible of that scene created over there, I made Dhruv leave from there and Nidhi ran from there and came to the stairs in front of the admin area where I and Dhruv were sitting, she came and shouted at Dhruv only without knowing the actual reason behind what Dhruv did, I tried to calm her down but she was in no mood to listen to anything, It hurt Dhruv that she is shouting on him without knowing the reason, Dhruv tried to make her understand about what happened there and why he did so but she didn't listened to anything, Nidhi left from there and we remained sitting there, Dhruv's heart got heavy and eyes filled with tears, I had seen Dhruv crying for the first time in the past  years since

I've known him, "Vipul I love her yaar, I couldn't hear anything inappropriate about her, they only commented on her physical appearance but I know her internally, I know her mentally and you listened na, what kind of language he was using for her, did I do anything wrong, I love her, she is my life, leave alone Nidhi how could I listen to those kind off disrespectful comment on any girl, how could I have silently listen to those kind of creepy comments on anyone, she didn't even listened to the reason and shouted on me" he cried his heart out and tears rolled down his eyes, I made him understand that he didn't do anything wrong but he did the right thing in the wrong way and wrong time, I told him that he should've shouted and talked to that boy in different manner and at some other place, as it suspended the event also, which was not good for the department and us also, we have ourselves made the arrangements and we destroyed it by ourselves, this is not good, you could've reacted in a different manner. I was consoling him when I received a call from Nidhi, she asked me to meet her at the canteen, I left for the canteen and asked Dhruv to go to the fest and apologize to the teacher and handle his work of managing the music system, he understood me and went to apologize for what he did and I went on to meet Nidhi in the canteen, she asked me all about the incidence and I explained her about what he happened there and asked her that it was not good what she did to her, I told her that at that moment when everyone spoke against Dhruv and was opposing him he hoped that she will be with him and support him by understanding all the things, but she did just opposite to this, she recognized her mistake and wanted to apologize to Dhruv as soon as possible, but she didn't got any chance to do so, she was being restless but she didn't got any chance to apologize, Dhruv was not talking to her properly, she knew Dhruv won't show any anger on her but deep down he was hurt, so she looked for an opportunity to apologize for the unwanted anger that she showed without listening to him, so she felt guilty, Dhruv remained busy in organizing the event and as soon as he got free it was time for the last event of the day, which was treasure hunt, the participation in the event was in team of four so I, Muskan, Nidhi and Dhruv formed a team and participated in the event, in the starting of the event we were given a list of items that needed to be collected in the given time frame, the team which came first will be the winner and will be awarded the winners price, our list of items were, 1)ATM slip 2)paper clips 3)a mirror 4)picture with a roadside vender 5)table tennis ball etc., there were a total of 10 items in the list. We saw the list and observed carefully all the items to be searched and figured out what we have with us and what do we need to arrange, we found ATM slips in Dhruv's wallet, mirror in Nidhi's bag, paper clips were there with Muskan and I had a stapler with me. So we needed to find only 6 items, we decided to distribute ourselves in 3 parts, Nidhi asked me to leave her with Dhruv so I went to look for Two things, muskan went for other two things and Nidhi and Dhruv together went for 2 items, Dhruv took out his phone to click a picture of the list so that if he finds any other thing he will collect that also, when he opened his phone's gallery to cross check the picture he found that he had a picture of himself with the chai waale bhaiya which he took on the fresher's party day when we went there after the event got over, so we needed to find only five things now, Dhruv and Nidhi went to arrange for the table tennis ball in the gym room in the parking area where table tennis was also there, Dhruv resisted to take Nidhi with her as he was hurt and did not wanted to face her alone, so he asked me to take Nidhi with me and he will arrange the ball alone but Nidhi signaled me that he wanted to be with him, so I made an excuse and left them together, Nidhi and Dhruv had to go together, Dhruv moved ahead and Nidhi followed him, Dhruv did not wanted to face her, but when they entered the parking area from the staircase on the canteen side corner Nidhi ran toward him and caught his hand from back, Nidhi knew that this was the opportunity she was looking for since the past few hour to apologize to Dhruv and forward her support to him, Dhruv tried to release his hands from her but she had decided to not let go of this opportunity, so she pulled Dhruv toward her and said,

"I know I have hurt you but I didn't knew the whole matter and I didn't liked that you slapped someone during my performance, it could have created a huge problem for us, I accept my mistake that I should've tried to understand the reason first and not shout on you unnecessarily but I didn't had control on me at that time" "please forgive me na, I love you na, don't do this to me, don't behave like this, please na"

Dhruv didn't uttered a single word till she completed and when she completed, he said, "did I said anything to you, If I am not saying anything to you than for what are you apologizing to me"

"but you are not behaving the same na" she replied

"leave me alone, I'll be normal in a while" he said

"why in a while? Why not now? Please Dhruv can't you forgive your love" she urged, she was in no mood to move from there till Dhruv became normal and forgave her for her mistake, so she tried and tried and after a few attempts Dhruv spoke,

"Nidhi you know na, the whole class is against me and you are the only one with whom I can expect a support, from whom I can cry my heart out, with whom I can calm myself, I wanted to tell you everything about what happened there, I wanted to tell you that I had guilt of raising my hands on that guy but at that time, I slapped him out of reflex, I wanted to talk to you, I expected you to understand me and show some support to me, but what you did, you shouted on me just like everyone, leave it yaar, I'll handle myself and will be normal soon".

Nidhi felt guilty and said, "I won't force you but I did it in reflex like you slapped him, even I couldn't have controlled myself at that moment, please forgive me"

She became a bit nervous and her eyes became heavy out of guilt, Dhruv can see anything but no tears in her eyes so all his anger, all his disappointment disappeared in a minute, and he hugged her, it was dark there so they were not visible moreover there was no-one around as it was the parking area and no-one came there. They hugged each other tight and forgot the purpose for which they had gone there, they hugged each other and forgot the world around when the sound of few feet and few people talking brought them in the real world and they separated from each other immediately, at that moment only Dhruv's phone rang and he took out his phone, muskan called him to ask if they have arranged the ball as she has completed her task and was waiting for everyone to join her in the ground where they had decided to meet after collecting all the items, "yeah we are just coming" replied Dhruv and hung up the call.

"come-on now we came here to arrange the table tennis ball and we forgot that only" said Dhruv they both laughed at each other and ran toward the gym room, took the ball and soon reached the place where Nidhi and I were waiting for them, "see, we both individually arranged 2 items each and you 2 together took longer than us to arrange a single item" I teased them, "Vipul bhai, our item was the toughest to find and you know na when we both are together it takes longer for anything to be done" Dhruv replied, "ohk, lets cross check the list with the items that we arranged and quickly submit them to win" hurried Muskan, we reached the table to submit the items and at that instant only another team also came and argued with the event in-charge to declare them as winners as they had come before us and we argued that we came first, we got the benefit of belonging of the same department and we won the treasure hunt, and we celebrated our victory, "the day belonged to us as we have won 2 of the four events today, let's celebrate" we all went to the food plaza to eat something where Sohail, Nikhil and megha joined us too. After sitting for a few minutes there, Sohail and Nikhil left on Sohail's bike and Muskan and megha left for the metro station and now only I, Nidhi and Dhruv were left there and we had only Dhruv's bike, so we decided that Dhruv will first Drop Nidhi near her home and then pick me up from Nidhi's bus stop where I'll reach by bus, Nidhi and Dhruv left from there and I boarded the bus, Nidhi held Dhruv tightly from the back and Dhruv rode slowly holding Nidhi's hand with one hand and riding with other, everything went well, Dhruv termed the incident as one more stretch in the two threads which tightened the knot between them, Nidhi loved this attitude of Dhruv that he always tried to look the positive aspect of everything and not the negative one, Dhruv Dropped Nidhi at the same point where he left her on the day they went to bangla sahib, he wanted a hug but Nidhi couldn't as it was her locality and someone might see them so, Dhruv understood her, they passed a smile to each other and Dhruv left, Dhruv was very happy that day, more than the problems that occurred that day, he had more moments to be happy, this joy in his heart lead to his careless and less attentive riding, he was on the road but his mind was roaming somewhere else, Dhruv was riding too fast and when he tried to overtake a bus in front of him, his bike got touched with the bonnet of a car and he met and accident, his bike got struck under the bus and a crowd gathered around him....

# CHAPTER:- 8
# THE CARE TAKER

"What happened? Where is he? Vo thik to hai na?" Nidhi came crying in the hospital as I had called her and informed that Dhruv met an accident while coming toward me after dropping her, she could not control herself and came running to the hospital immediately after getting the news. She was so restless and panicked that she could barely contain her tears and urge to see Dhruv, I informed her that the doctor is putting bandage on his wounds and they needed to examine his legs by getting an x-ray as he was not able to move his right leg properly, he had scratches and sprains all over his right side of the body as he fell on that side and slid with his bike to a distance. When I saw doctor coming out of the room for some work I entered the room immediately and Nidhi came with me too, I asked what did the doctor say about the wounds and the proceedings to be done ahead, Dhruv was about to say something when Nidhi broke out and started crying heavily, she could not contain her pain of her love in pain, she couldn't even hug him as it would hurt his wounds, she sat there only near Dhruv's legs and started crying heavily she could barely manage to speak a word, she was just crying and crying, Dhruv spoke and tried to pacify her,

"Are beta I am ok, these are just sprains and would soon heal up, they don't cause pain, just keep calm, the small wounds will heal up soon, don't worry about them, if you'll cry like this how can I stand these wounds and stand strong, please keep calm, for me."

He was saying these things when his dad entered in the room with the doctor, I had called his dad too and informed him about the accident, his dad saw Nidhi crying there and me standing at a side, he raised his brows but didn't said anything as he was also worried for his son, he asked the doctor about his injuries and the doctor explained him that Dhruv had fractured his right leg and it has to be plastered and Dhruv has to be given proper bed rest for atleast 2 weeks so that his bones could heel, it came as a shock for all of us as we had not thought of such a severe injury, Nidhi got worried about him and before his father could speak she asked the doctor, "sir, is there any other major injury or this fracture only?" Dhruv held her from behind and said, "Nidhi papa ji is talking to the doctor, let him talk", he signaled me to take Nidhi out of the room and calm her down, I did the same, I took Nidhi outside and made her sit on the chairs in front of the room and tried to calm her down, she was not ready to listen anything and just sit in front of Dhruv but I somehow managed to keep her out, we waited outside for them to come out so that we could return back home, it was around 6:30 in the evening and Nidhi had already received many calls from her home but Nidhi was not ready to leave Dhruv until she sees him ok, soon uncle ji came holding Dhruv while Dhruv was walking on one feet I got up and held Dhruv from other side to provide him some support. He kept his hand on our shoulders and walked to his father's car, Nidhi followed us and asked Dhruv to please take care of himself, Dhruv's father answered Nidhi and said "you don't worry beta ji his mom and I am there to take care of him, you also get back home, it's too late and your family would be worried about you", his father handed Dhruv's bike's keys to me and asked me to Drop Nidhi home and drive properly, he took Dhruv home, while I dropped Nidhi and then went to his home to return the bike keys, I parked his bike and went into his room, where he was chatting with Nidhi, I sat on the chair beside his bed and asked if he is ok or still having pain, he kept his phone aside and showed me all his scratches and wounds, his right side was nearly completely scratched he had bruises on his shoulder and face, a deep wound on the knee, scratched elbows and a fractured leg, luckily he had worn his helmet which protected his head to get an injury otherwise the situation could have been worst, I asked him if his dad asked him about Nidhi? He nodded in affirmation then I asked him about his answer about Nidhi, he said he told his father that Nidhi is our classmate and a good friend and is very close to me and Dhruv so she came there to see him, I wished him a speedy recovery and left his home and reached my home as my mother was also tensed when I told her about the accident due to which I would be late, after I left his home he started talking to Nidhi again and she was requesting Dhruv to let her come to his home for some time but Dhruv was refusing as he didn't wanted to bother her but at the end he had to agree with Nidhi and let her come to his home to see him, Dhruv told his mom about Nidhi coming to see him when she came in her room to give him dinner and medicine as he wanted to inform prior to her coming so that her mother can get comfortable about her.

The next morning Nidhi met me at her bus stop and gave me her assignment that has to be submitted in the college on that day only, and he took a cab and reached Dhruv's home, Dhruv had asked her to come after 10 'O' clock as by that time his father would have left for office and only his mom would be there, who would not say anything moreover she will welcome her whole heartedly, she reached his home and called him to ask his mom to open the door, his mom opened the door and welcomed Nidhi, Nidhi touched her feet and took her blessings and asked her for Dhruv, his mom took Nidhi with her to Dhruv's room and sat there with them, Dhruv introduced her to his mom, "mom she is that Nidhi about whom I used to tell you, she is the sweetest friend I have, we are friends since day 1 of our college", his mom replied, "till today I had just heard about you finally I saw you, he keeps on talking about you only" Nidhi kept quiet and smiled, "I'll bring something for you, you guys carry on with your talks" she said and left her room, Nidhi saw Dhruv lying on the bed and noticed all the wounds that he got the previous day in the accident, which she could not see the day before, she held his hand and asked, "are you ok?", "I am very much fine as you are there with me" he replied.

She saw his plastered leg and felt a deep grieve for him as he had to suffer such pain for some days now, she enquired him about his medicine, which he had not taken till then, "have you eaten something or not?" she asked "yaar mom has not let my mouth to take any rest, she is bringing something every now and then and I am eating everything" he replied, they were talking when his mom entered the room with juice and water for them, "take this" she forwarded the tray toward her, "aunty ji there is no need for all this, I've not come here for any kind of hostility, I had come to see him only, please don't bother yourself for these things," said Nidhi, "this is nothing beta, just take this", Nidhi remained there for a few hours and kept on talking to Dhruv and his mother, Dhruv told his mother about a few funny incidences of the college, and they laughed together, Nidhi sat there until when I returned from college and asked her to go as she hadn't told at her home that she'll be late so she should reach on time. She left from there, greeting aunty ji and asking Dhruv to take care, aunty ji asked her to come whenever she wanted as she had told her that Dhruv was not letting her come there, so she decided to come there regularly till Dhruv gets healed up. Nidhi reached a bit late to her home that day and was under suspicious eyes, her mom asked her the reason for being late and why was he not picking up the phone, Nidhi remembered that she had kept her phone on silent and hadn't seen it for a while now, "mom, I didn't saw my hone it was lying in my bag and I didn't had my bag with me, sorry", "ok fine, but where were you till now, you never came this much late since you started going college, Nidhi didn't wanted to lie to her mother but she couldn't tell the complete truth also, so she smartly told her mother that she is joining the theatre society in the college for which she was giving auditions today and after that she went to see Dhruv, she had already introduced Dhruv as her good friend and had told her mother that Dhruv had met an accident, so she told her mom that she had been to Dhruv's place to see him and she cleared her path for the coming days by saying, "mom please don't worry about me coming late, because I might have to stay back at college after my classes for a few days for the society meeting and practice", her mom didn't say anything and asked her to freshen up and eat something. Nidhi went to her room and started talking to Dhruv and told her about what happened when she came back home, Dhruv again urged her not to bother herself unnecessarily but Nidhi had something else in her mind. Nidhi used to go to college first and then go to his home after finishing the lectures in the college so that she does not lack behind in her study, Nidhi slowly became comfortable with his mom and didn't hesitated in saying or asking her anything, in absence of his mother she gave everything which Dhruv needed, she fed him with her hands, she wiped of his face, she gave him medicines, she even changed her bandages, she applied ointments on his wounds, she took care of him in best possible way, she used to teach her all the lessons that were being taught in the classes so that he does misses the studies and his work load does not pile up on him.

One day her mom wanted to go out as she had some work. so, she asked her to take care of Dhruv till she returns and left, Nidhi shut the door behind her and went to the kitchen to take some fruits from the refrigerator to give to Dhruv, she went in his room and sat beside him and cut the fruits and made him eat them, Nidhi and Dhruv were alone in their home that day, Dhruv held her hands and said, "you take care of me like my mother, you are doing everything for me, how will I be able to thank you for all this"

"you need not to thank me for anything as I am not doing anything for you, I am doing all this for me only, as it is very painful for me to see you in pain, I can bear anything but not any kind of wound on you, I can't see you in pain, so I am doing all this to make myself happy" she replied and smiled

"you are so sweet yaar, I love you" he said

"I love you too, now don't stretch yourself for long just lie down"

Dhruv laid himself on the bed and pulled Nidhi toward her, "it's your home baby" she said, "but no one is there" he replied, Nidhi bent toward him, her hair came forward and covered his face, he wiped her hair from his face, and saw her face, she was kneeling on her and slowly she came closer to him and rested her face on his chest, she could hear his heartbeat, he hugged her and rested his chin on her head, they remained in that position talking to each other and spending some quality time together, "jaldi se thik ho jaao fir hum ghoomne challenge" she said, "just a few days more, this plaster will be cut off and I'll be able to walk freely" he said and kissed her forehead, Nidhi came up kissed his cheeks and smiled, "now leave me, aunty ji will be coming anytime soon" she said, Dhruv left her and she came back to her position siting on the chair beside her, "so you want anything else" she asked, "just a kiss" he naughtily replied, "I am asking about anything to eat or drink baby" "don't fly high in the sky, first you need to get well, focus on that and not on me" she replied smartly. The doorbell rang, his mother had returned back, Nidhi ran toward the door and opened the door and welcomed her in, it was time for her to leave. Nidhi left for her home and this continued till the time Dhruv became fit to come to college.

Dhruv started coming to college but in spite of Nidhi teaching him a few lesson she lagged behind in submitting the assignments and doing the practical file work and completing his work. So, he had a work load on him which was to be completed within a weak as the semester was about to end and the college was about to close for preparatory leave, he tried to complete his work in the free time in the college and Nidhi always sat beside him, helping him in making the diagrams and understanding the basic concepts, Nidhi also helped him in completing the assignments, while Dhruv used to complete one of his work Nidhi wrote the other one, she also took some work to her home and submitted it in the college the next day, apart from all this curricular work Nidhi also took him to the doctor for check-ups and took care that Dhruv do not put pressure on his leg, she even tied the crepe bandage on his leg so that he can heel fast, she made him eat healthy and nutritious food so that he can recover all the loss due to his injuries. With all this support and help from Nidhi, Dhruv completed all his work on time before the college closed.

The college closed and we remained at our home preparing for the examination, like always I and Dhruv sat at his home and studies together, Dhruv helped me with the concepts but sometime I also helped him in those topics which he missed studying the college due to his injuries, all the things in our exam preparation were like ever before but there was a change that Nidhi also joined us somedays, she was comfortable in coming to his home as she was known to his mother and by this way she helped us in preparing for the examination. The exams went well with our preparation and the semester ended.

It was time for a long semester break this time as the exams ended on 24$^{th}$ of May and the college were to reopen on 21$^{st}$ of July, so Nidhi went to her hometown to spend the holidays but unlike the previous holidays, Dhruv and Nidhi used to talk to each other a lot and share each and everything happened in their life with each other.

Dhruv told Nidhi that Sohail was about to contest the college elections that year, and he has called him to college in these holidays to assist the new students coming to take admissions in the college, this way they will be able to interact with the students and get there support on behalf of their help in there admission, Dhruv was a helpful guy and didn't not refused to help anybody to the extent up to which he can do something, so he asked Nidhi to come back soon as he was going to college and it was a chance to meet, but Nidhi could not come as she had her reservation for her return journey and it was of 13th of July, so she could not come. They remained talking to each other but when Dhruv started going to college he didn't talked to her during the time he remained in college and gradually there conversations rapped up to a particular time in the day, but Dhruv always tried to talk to her whenever he got even a few minutes to talk. They talked and talked and waited for the college to reopen so that they could meet.

Nishant Jha

# CHAPTER:- 9
# NEW FRIEND

Dhruv had started going to college on the days of cutoffs so that he could interact with the students and become friend with them so that at the time of the elections he could make his friend win the elections by asking the new students to vote in his favor, he made many friends those days, many took his phone number so that they can contact him whenever they find any difficulty about the college curriculum and any other issue, he happily gave his number as this was the opportunity for him to become friends with more and more number of students.

It was the third cutoff when a girl interacted with him for quite a long time, she looked somehow attracted toward his personality, Dhruv helped her in filling the form, arranging all her documents and guiding her the way to the room where all these things were to be submitted, but she urged Dhruv to accompany her to the room and assist her in the proceedings ahead, Dhruv couldn't deny her request and walked with her, on the way toward the room Dhruv introduced her to the college building, telling about each and everything they were passing by, she asked Dhruv about the faculties and the decorum of the college, Dhruv told her that in-spite of being an of campus college it is one of the best college of Delhi university in terms of studies and academic curriculum, soon they reached room no 113 which was actually the physics lab, the professor sitting there knew Dhruv very well so he greeted the professor and made her submit the documents and complete all the required formalities, she asked Dhruv for the way toward the canteen as she was feeling hungry, Dhruv guided her the way and left from there to the room where all his other friends were sitting, a few moments later that girl came to Dhruv and asked for his number in the name of any future assistance regarding the college and any other work, Dhruv gave his number and continued with his help to others, he didn't paid much attention to this and returned home that day.

A few days later while Dhruv was busy cleaning his room he received a call from an unknown number, he first ignored the call and thought to call back after sometime when done with the work, but he got another call from the same number so, he couldn't ignore that this time, he picked up the call,

"Hello" he said

"hello, am I talking to Dhruv"

"yup, may I know whose speaking from the other end"

"it's Apurva this side"

"sorry Apurva, I can't recognize you"

"I am the girl whom you helped in the college, you went with me to submit my documents and I took your number while leaving"

Dhruv remembered that girl as she possessed some characteristics like Nidhi and so he said, "oh yeah, gotcha, how are you?"

"I am doing great, how are you?" she asked

"I am also good, so tell me how may I help you"

"yaar actually I am not from Delhi so I require an accommodation in near the college to continue with the college"

"you should've filled the form for hostel"

"I am not a dumbo dude, I had filled the form but didn't got the hostel, so I need a PG now"

Dhruv liked her outspoken behavior and the way she talked,

"ohk ohk, so how may I help you with this, I am limited to college only"

"you need to help me in finding a PG for me, I don't know how but you got to help me, you told me that day that you'll help me with anything in future"

"I can provide you the contact of my friend who lives in the PG nearby he might be having knowledge about this"

"why don't you talk to your friend yourself and ask him about this" "ohk, fine. I'll talk to him and get back to you shortly"

They had this conversation and hung up the call, Dhruv called Amit who lived in a PG to enquire him about the PG and gather all the information regarding the PG so that he can inform Apurva about it and assist her to get the PG so that she doesn't faces any problem in getting an accommodation.

He received a text on WhatsApp that evening from Apurva's number asking him about the PG, Dhruv gave her all the options of PG's available near the college and their charges and services available in those PG's so that she can decide from those and choose the appropriate for her according to her needs, after knowing about the PG's she started to talk to him casually like a friend and started sharing her life with him and they became friends, Dhruv told her about Nidhi and she also told him about his boyfriend, in a matter of just one conversation the equations matched and Apurva felt attached to Dhruv.

Dhruv told Nidhi about this incidence and Nidhi did not liked that any other girl talked to him like this, Dhruv identified the insecurity in Nidhi's voice and so explained her, "don't be insecure baby, I am your and only yours, no one can replace you, I love you and only you and moreover I had told her about you and she also has a boyfriend so don't worry about her". Nidhi wanted to ask Dhruv to not talk to her but she didn't want to sound like she is putting restrictions in his life, so she didn't say anything, but deep down she was not comfortable with this. Dhruv got an idea that Nidhi didn't liked this and hence decided to not talk to Apurva more frequently.

Apurva texted Dhruv but he tried to ignore her for a while but when he saw her message in the notification bar which read, "hey, I've come to Delhi to finalize my PG accommodation, can you please meet me and help me with that" he could not resist himself to help her out, he called her and asked her to meet him the college main gate, from where he will take her to the PG's and make her choose the suitable, in the next  5 minutes she was there and called Dhruv informing him that she had reached and was waiting for him there, Dhruv informed Sohail and came running to the college door to find Apurva waiting for him sitting on the walls, Dhruv waved at her and she waved him back, Dhruv asked her to lets go to the PG's near the college, she said,

"hey dude, how rude are you? a girl was waiting for you in this hot sunny day, you are not even asking for something and kya hum chal ke jaane waale hai ye PG dekhne? Yaar I can't walk under this sun"

"oh sorry, what would you like to have, shikanji or ice-cream?" he asked

"what if I would like to have both, won't you get me both the things together?" she joked

"why not? Let me change the question then, what would you like to have first, a shikanji or an ice-cream?"

Dhruv and Apurva took a glass of Shikanji each and then he bought an ice-cream cone for her.

"ohk, gentleman now how will we go?"

Dhruv showed her his bike keys and excused himself to take out his bike from where he parked it, Apurva sat with him and they went to look for the PG's around the college about which Dhruv had enquired, he showed her all the PG's in Vasundhara enclave and asked If she finalized one or does she require to have a look at one or two more,

"although I can choose one from these but I'll be catching the bus back home in the evening so we have much time left, you can take me to some more places if you know more", she said

After this Dhruv rode her to a PG which was in Mayur Vihar phase-3 which was a bit far from the college, she saw it and finalized that one at the same instant and even paid the advance amount and told the PG owner that she will soon come with her stuff, after that Dhruv asked her if she was hungry and want to eat something. She thanked Dhruv for her help and asked him to take her to a food point, she told him that she'll be paying the bills on the food point but Dhruv  didn't ate anything on someone else's money ever so he said either he will pay the bill or if she wants to pay something then they will Dutch the bill, so they agreed on going Dutch and then he rode her back to the food plaza near the college, they had a plate of Chilly potato and a cold drink for them and left from there. Dhruv dropped her to the Anand Vihar bus depot and made her board the bus back home and asked her to text or call him when she reached, Dhruv showed her a gesture of care by asking her to do so, Dhruv felt somehow attached to her after spending the complete day with her, as soon as reached home, he received a call from Nidhi on his phone, he told her how Apurva came today and how the day went, Nidhi's voice slowed on listening her name again from Dhruv, Dhruv tried to comfort her, "baby, she is a sweet girl, she is as outspoken as you are, she is cute and doesn't keeps anything in her mind, she speaks whatever she feels, she is a nice girl overall and you don't worry about her in my life, she can be nothing but a friend in my life, she is like muskan and megha, they are also my friend na, I talk to them also but you don't worry about me talking to them, treat her like another friend, she is just another friend of mine" but Nidhi had not met her yet and how can she believe any girl, if she is trying to steal her Dhruv, and the way Dhruv was telling about her Nidhi felt a bit insecure but she didn't say anything to him.

"baby you are sounding worried, if you want, I won't talk to her, I had tried to avoid her since the first day, but she came today just relying on me that's why I went with her" said Dhruv

"No No, it's okay, I don't know that girl but I believe you, you are mine and mine only. I trust you" she replied,

Dhruv became happy that Nidhi had accepted her as friend and understood his friendship with Apurva, they shared there day with each other, they talked for around an hour and when they hung up the call, Dhruv saw some messages from Apurva, it read,

"hey dude, I reached home"

"I had called you to inform but you were busy on some other call"

"thank you for all you did today"

"will catch up with you soon, when I'll come with my luggage"

Dhruv could not avoid her this time, and replied to her messages,

"oh okay, actually I was talking to Nidhi, no need for thanks, I can do this much for you ohk, take some rest, you might have got tired with the hectic day, will talk later"

Dhruv talked to her more frequently now and soon they become good friends, he introduced Apurva to me also and I also became friends with her. Dhruv was not going to college now as the all the cut-offs were over and hence all of us were waiting for 21$^{st}$ of July, so that the college reopens and we meet each other, Dhruv was the one waiting the most curiously as she wanted to meet Nidhi badly and was excited to introduce Nidhi to the new friend...

# CHAPTER:- 10
# THE MUTUAL FRIENDSHIP

It was the day for which everyone was waiting, everyone had their share of excitement about the reopening of college, Nidhi and Dhruv were excited that they will get to meet each other after so long, they were waiting for this day since day zero of the vacations as they were not able to meet during the break this time, I was excited that I'll get to see new girls in college as my juniors to pleasure my eyes, Apurva was excited for her college life to begin, Sohail was excited that he can now be the poster boy of the college by contesting the elections. In between these excitements Nidhi and Apurva were excited to meet each other also, Apurva was looking to meet the person about whom she has always heard from Dhruv, she wanted to see the beauty that Dhruv described about her, she wanted to see the lucky girl who has got a partner like Dhruv in her life, on the other hand Nidhi wanted to meet the girl whom his Dhruv could not avoid talking to, she wanted to meet the girl who became friend with her Dhruv so easily. So, it was a day full of excitement for everyone.

Dhruv called me, "hey Vipul come fast dude, we are already late, Nidhi will wait for us and we should not keep her waiting for long" he could talk about Nidhi in his home as Nidhi was known to everyone in his home, "just coming dude, it's not about keeping Nidhi waiting but about your excitement, you can't control yourself for long now" I replied and reached his home in the next five minutes and we left for college, he called Nidhi to tell that we have left and she should leave accordingly and meet us at her bus stop, as soon as he cut the call his phone rang, his screen read Apurva, she was calling him to know about the time he would be coming to college, he told her that we have left from home will reach the college in an hour or so. "ohk will catch you there" she said and hung up the call. Soon we reached Nidhi's bus stop and found Nidhi waiting there, Nidhi and Dhruv could not control their emotions there and hugged each other tightly, and remained locked in each other's arms till I broke the silence, "the bus is coming dude, we need to board this bus" Nidhi and Dhruv left each other and just held there hand in hand, the bus stopped in front of us and we boarded the bus, we saw some seats vacant in the end so Dhruv and Nidhi jumped to sit there and I waited near the bus conductor to take the tickets, Nidhi and Dhruv looked at each other like the sun looks toward the horizon, like a bird looks the sky, like a person got the treasure, their eyes were glowing and they couldn't avoid looking at each other, I came and stood in front of them to guard them from the eyes of other people standing in the bus, soon we reached college and took pics of our time table from the notice board, we didn't had any class till 11:30 that day and it was just 9 'O' clock we had a long two and a half hours to spare, so we decided to go to the ground and sit there for a while, we had reached the ground and were looking for a shaded area to sit in when Dhruv received another call from Apurva, she had also reached college and asked for our location in the college, Dhruv told her that we have just come to ground and so she can come there if she wants, she asked him to wait there as she was also coming to meet them, Dhruv asked us to wait for a minute for her to come, "haan ji, let his friend come first, the group is incomplete without her" Nidhi teased Dhruv, I laughed with her, soon we saw a girl in yellow suit coming toward us, "is she the one?" asked Nidhi, "yup" replied Dhruv. Apurva came toward us and shook hands with Dhruv and me and hugged Nidhi, "oh my god, I mean OMG, finally I saw you and you are exactly like what Dhruv has told me, I have heard a lot about you from him, he doesn't has anything to talk about except you, Nidhi is this, Nidhi is that, Nidhi does this, Nidhi does that, Nidhi likes this, Nidhi likes that, none of his sentences completes without taking your name atleast once." It was an awkward moment for Nidhi, "achchha ye mere baare me bhi baat krte hai, I thought bas mujhse hi aapki baate karte hai" they talked to each other and they both didn't needed to be introduced to each other as Dhruv had already told them many things about each other, they talked there for a few moments till I interrupted "are we standing here only or can we sit somewhere" and then we went on to sit near the volleyball court where we always found shade.

Nidhi and Apurva became comfortable with each other and talked like they knew each other since a long time, Apurva told her how Dhruv helped her in doing all the things in the admission procedure and how he helped her in getting a PG for her, he did all the things selflessly without expecting anything in return. She was telling Nidhi everything as if Nidhi didn't knew her Dhruv and his behavior and nature, moreover Dhruv had told each and everything to her about how he helped Apurva and how he spend his days, what all he did, and how many friends he made, with how many people he interacted to, and specifically each and everything about Apurva. It showed Apurva's childish behavior which made Nidhi comfortable with her, I asked if someone wants to have tea as I badly needed it so everyone including Apurva raised their hands, so in total I needed to bring four cups from the canteen so, I needed to take someone with me so I asked, "who is coming with me to bring tea from the canteen?" Dhruv said "Vipul, I am coming with you dude, vaise bhi itni der se hum yaha hai hi nahi, they both are complete in themselves" and stood up to come with me but Apurva pulled him down and said, "oh drama queen baitho apni Nidhi k saath jaa rahi hu mai" and she accompanied me to the canteen.

"she is a sweet girl." Said Nidhi to Dhruv about Apurva

"I told you, you were unnecessarily being insecure about her" said Dhruv

"she is sweet doesn't means I shouldn't be insecure about her" Nidhi replied

"so, what do you want, I shouldn't talk to her" he asked

"see Dhruv I am not doubting you or her, but you know na what you mean to me, I can't share you with anyone." She replied

"ok fine I'll do what makes you happy" he said and smiled pulling her cheeks

They were smiling at this when Apurva and me reached there with the cups of tea, "what's going on lovebirds? What is there which is making you smile so wide" Apurva teased them,

"nothing special, come sit" Nidhi took the tea from her hand and asked us to sit.

We sat there and sipped the tea, and talked there for hours until the sunlight came towards us and hence, we had to move from there, we stood and moved to the canteen and took the corner bench there,

"don't you have class today?" asked Nidhi to Apurva

"no actually I had a lab from 08:30-12:30 but it will start from the next week so I am free till 12:30" answered Apurva

"I hope I am not disturbing you; I can leave if you want me to" Apurva said in a low tone

"oh no no, you are not disturbing us at all, moreover I want you to stay with me today as muskan and megha are not there with me and for me you are a nice company to be with, I didn't mean that just keep sitting here only" explained Nidhi

Dhruv didn't wanted to be in this and doesn't wanted to sound like he is not liking her company there and so he asked Apurva that she can be with them anytime she wanted to be but Nidhi didn't liked this as she believed that she had explained to Apurva properly and Dhruv needed not to get into this unnecessarily, it was around 11:15 and we needed to get to the class as we had our class from 11:30, so we decided to leave from there and go to the class but Apurva didn't had any class so she decided to come with us till our class and from there she'll go to the library and then will go to her class at 12:30 , so we started walking toward our classroom, on the way toward the classroom Dhruv received a call from Sohail who asked him that he needs some help and hence asked Dhruv not to go into the class, and come with him to the Vasundhara plaza, Dhruv couldn't deny his request to help him so he decided to not attend the class and take the notes from Nidhi after the class, Apurva asked Dhruv if she can come with him as she has not taken any class yet so, she would not be having anything to read in the library and it would be boring for her there, this faded the colors on Nidhi's face but no-one noticed as she was good at hiding her emotions, Dhruv didn't said anything but he didn't wanted to say no to Apurva and he didn't wanted to hurt Nidhi too, so he chose silence and let Nidhi answer her, seeing this dilemma on Dhruv's face Apurva understood the problem and looked toward Nidhi and said,

"I hope you don't mind di"

"yeah you should go with him, you'll get a company otherwise you would have got bored in the library" Nidhi replied

I can sense the insecurity on Nidhi's face and the way she answered but I didn't say anything. Dhruv left for the admin area where Sohail had called him and Apurva accompanied him, Nidhi didn't wanted to sound like Dhruv does everything with her permission and didn't wanted to seem like she is not allowing Dhruv to be friend with Apurva or any other girl, but she didn't liked that Apurva was always there with Dhruv, even when she is not around, she trusted Dhruv but a sense of insecurity always prevailed in her head, she was helpless that she couldn't do anything.

We went for the class and remained in the class till 1:30 as we had two classes back to back but Nidhi was not at all attentive in the class as her mind was roaming somewhere else, so I made all the notes so I can provide her with the notes, we marked our attendance and came out and called Dhruv, he asked us to come to the food plaza, as he was there only, Nidhi and I walked toward the food plaza to find Dhruv and Apurva sitting there waiting for us, Nidhi was shocked to see Apurva there, she thought that she might have gone to her class at 12:30 she came to know that her class has been cancelled so she remained with Dhruv only in this time.

Nidhi became somehow upset with this and didn't sat there and excused herself to go to home, Dhruv ran behind her and asked her, "what happened baby? You are behaving strangely today, are you upset because of Apurva? Baby I told you I'll do whatever makes you happy, I didn't even agree for her to be with me during this time, you only asked her to be with me. Baby I really don't want to hurt you, I'll try to make distance with her too, but please don't do like this na, even you know her she is a nice girl and won't be coming between us, please don't do like this and come with us, we will just take a cold drink and move, come na otherwise she'll not feel good, please"

He tried to convince Nidhi but she didn't agreed and hence left for her home, Dhruv came smiling toward us, hiding his thoughts behind the smile but I knew him since a long time now so I easily identified that all is not good between them, even Apurva smell something fishy and asked Dhruv if everything is ohk, Dhruv smiled and didn't say anything, "so what would you like to have?" he asked us "don't flip my question please, why did Nidhi left from here?" said Apurva in strong tone "arey nothing dude, chill. She was not feeling ok due to this hot weather and left because of this only." Answered Dhruv

Apurva did not said anything further and kept quiet, Dhruv ordered a plate of singapuri noodles and cold drinks for us, no-one spoke a word and left from there after completing the food.

These things continued for a while, Apurva always remained with Dhruv when not in class, Dhruv was not able to spend time with Nidhi as he used to remain with Sohail and did not attended many classes also, Dhruv utilized his image and got the attendance marked so that he doesn't face any difficulty ahead due to the attendance, and always remained here and there, sometimes, campaigning with Sohail, sometime interacting with the juniors, sometime writing some applications, sometimes getting the work done for juniors, overall he didn't remained with us or spend time with Nidhi for about one month. But Apurva remained with him most of the time. These things annoyed Nidhi and she remained very irritated this days, Dhruv talked to her in the evening on call but he didn't came to meet her for once in college, she even told Apurva to not remain with him, because he didn't wanted to be spotted with anyone by the other candidates in front of Sohail, because they may target the one with Dhruv and may threaten them to restrict Dhruv from getting close to other students. Dhruv even explained this reason to Nidhi, Nidhi asked him to leave all this and become the same Dhruv which he was before this semester. Nidhi didn't want anything just her Dhruv as he was, but Dhruv was a man of his words and cannot leave Sohail now. He was there with Sohail in all her steps and had promised to be with him throughout.

These things created a gap between the two and nothing remained same between them, Dhruv made all his efforts to make Nidhi understand and balance his life, he even clearly told Apurva not to remain with him, but nothing happened in their favor, Nidhi remained insecure and irritated by this.

# CHAPTER:- 11
# THE LAST ATTEMPT

Dhruv remained busy with the campaigning and all other things with Sohail but deep inside he always wanted to be with Nidhi and spend some time with her but he was not able to do so, Nidhi remained alone always, she didn't talk to anybody, she was very much disappointed with whatever had happened in the past few days. Dhruv even tried to explain her that we will be normal again and we will be the same again just give him a few days more till the elections gets completed, but Nidhi was not able to understand these things.

On one side Nidhi was having many thoughts in her mind about Dhruv, she had in her mind that Dhruv had changed, her Dhruv don't loves her the way he did, he didn't wants to spend time with her, he restricts her from meeting him, he gives more attention to Apurva and more such thoughts, on the other hand Dhruv's point of views and thoughts were completely different on this he wanted to spend time with her but he was not able to because he did not wanted to create any kind of kiosk in her life, he wanted to give more attention to her but he didn't attended class those days and didn't wanted Nidhi to miss her classes so they didn't had any time to be together, he was never keeping Apurva over Nidhi as his priority, but there was a communication gap between the two so they had a difference of thoughts between them, when Dhruv got to know about the thought in Nidhi's mind about Apurva he decided to tell Apurva about this and ask her to not spend much time with him and not to remain with him as her Nidhi don't like this and is being insecure about her.

While coming back home in the evening Dhruv called Apurva to talk to her about this,

"hey, how come you are calling this time?" Apurva said on picking the phone,

"actually, I wanted to talk to you about something" replied Dhruv

"is it about Nidhi?" Apurva asked, she had an idea that Dhruv is somehow disturbed with his relationship and somewhere she might be the reason behind this.

Dhruv didn't say anything

"are its ok, tell me kya baat hai, you can talk to me about anything dude" Apurva comforted Dhruv

"yaar actually nothing is going right between us, you've seen that I am not able to give her time, I am not able to spend time with her, but you've seen na I try to make time out of this to talk to her, but she is not able to understand and is thinking much unnecessarily, I tried to make her understand and is just repeating the thing that I am not the same Dhruv which I used to be, I have changed for her, she even said that she is no more important to me, Apurva what should I do, I am not able to understand anything, please suggest me something, what should I do?" said Dhruv

Apurva felt in his voice that he wanted to say something but was not able to say, so she said, "is this only thing you wanted to say or is there something else because I've been with you these days and I know these things, I'll say please give her and yourself a bit space and time, everything will be fine soon, I know how much you love her and i know how much she loves you, you both will be fine soon, the thing is the situations are not good these days, just wait a bit and don't panic, everything will be fine."

"Apurva I don't know how to say this but you know Nidhi thinks that I have prioritized you before her and I am ignoring her because of you, I don't have anything in mind about you and I know you understand me and would try to know why I am saying this, can you please maintain a bit distance from me, till the time everything becomes normal between me and her, please try to understand" said Dhruv

"are its ok you need not to hesitate about this, I won't come with you from now on and will try not to talk to you as far as possible" replied

Apurva, this thing hurt her but she didn't say anything, and she tried to remain calm and neutral,

"yaar I don't know what to do and what not to do, please don't get me wrong and we are friends and will always be, you can talk to me anytime you want and can ask me for anything you need but for this time let me try to make Nidhi comfortable please" said Dhruv trying to keep Apurva comfortable and not to sound too rude on her

"ji, I know this that you are my go-to person whenever I need you, and we'll be same always, the same level of craziness, same strength of bond and the same you and me" said Apurva and smiled

"yeah, for sure" said Dhruv

"anything else I can help you with?" asked Apurva

"can you talk to Nidhi for once and try to make her comfortable and make her understand that there is nothing like she is thinking" asked Dhruv to Apurva

"ok, will talk to her tomorrow, now just chill and don't worry, everything will be ok"

Dhruv thanked Apurva and hung up the call.

Dhruv kept thinking about this the entire way back home and wanted to talk to Nidhi so he tried calling Nidhi but Nidhi didn't picked up the call, he tried calling again but this time also the call went unanswered, he then dropped a message on Nidhi's phone, "call me when you are free, we need to talk" Nidhi saw the message and left it as she was not in a mood to talk, Dhruv was being very much restless and wanted to talk to her badly but she was not in a mood, she was irritated with all the things that had happened these days, so she didn't replied the message. Dhruv checked the status of the message and found that Nidhi had read the message at that time when he sent the message but didn't replied, so his restlessness increased, he wanted to talk to her badly but the situations has become worst day by day and he didn't had an idea about what is happening and what will happen now, but it was clear in her mind that he didn't wanted to lose his Nidhi at any cost. Dhruv didn't knew what to do ahead so he called me, "Vipul, bhai I want to talk to you yaar, Nidhi is not talking to me, I had called her but she didn't pick up my phone and when I texted her, she saw the message and didn't even replied, yaar Vipul I don't want to lose her, please help me bhai, she is not talking to me, I know she is furious on me but you know yaar what I am going through these days, what she means to me, Vipul please help me dude, please help me, please talk to Nidhi yaar, please try to make her understand, bhai please talk to her," and he broke,

"Dhruv calm down yaar, I'll talk to her, please don't do like this, I don't like you being so much helpless, I'll talk to her na, please calm down" I tried to comfort her

"Vipul, can you please take her on conference call and make me talk to her for once" Dhruv requested me to call Nidhi

"just wait I'll try to call her, lets see if she picks up the call or not"

I put him on hold and called Nidhi, she picked up the call in one ring

"Haan Vipul, howz you?" said Nidhi

"I am ohk, how are you?" I replied and put the call on conference

"hello, is she on call?" said Dhruv

"yes, she is" "Nidhi Dhruv is on call please talk to her" I said on call

Nidhi cut the call immediately on knowing that Dhruv was there on call, this made Dhruv more restless and he became silent and broke down,

"Dhruv please keep calm dude, I'll talk to her na, please give me time till tomorrow, I'll meet her tomorrow and talk to her, everything will be fine" I tried to calm him down but his condition was not that he could understand anything, he kept on crying and crying and was not able to control himself.

"ohk, dude fine, I'll control myself but please talk to her tomorrow" Dhruv somehow managed to say this and hung up the call,

I knew that he was not ok and will not say anything to anyone but I knew deep inside he was not able to control himself, he kept on tossing and turning on the bed the whole night and didn't slept the whole night waiting for the next day hoping that Apurva and I'll talk to Nidhi and everything will be fine.

The next day Dhruv came to my home with a smile on his face, hiding his pain behind that wide smile, he asked me to talk to Nidhi and left with Sohail, who had come to pick him up to go somewhere, he tried calling Nidhi but she didn't answered the call again, he didn't wanted to show anything on his face so that Sohail could not identify the pain in his heart but everyone in our group including muskan, megha, Sohail and Nikhil knew about Dhruv and Nidhi, everyone knew that there are misunderstanding between the two and everyone believed that they'll be fine soon once they clear out the misunderstanding and sort out the things by sitting together, everyone knew that both of them had made efforts to be together but the situations were against them and nothing went in their favor. Dhruv left with Sohail and they dropped me at the college before leaving for some work, I went to the college and called Nidhi but she didn't pick my call too. So, I looked for her in the our classroom but she was not there, I sneaked into other classes also in which we used to sit somedays, I sent a girl of our class in girls common room also to check if she was there but I found her nowhere so I tried calling her again but she didn't took the call again, I asked in my class if anyone has seen her to confirm that she has come to college, megha and muskan told me that she has attended the first class and then left the classroom and went out alone, they told me that she was a bit tensed and when they asked to accompany her she requested them to let her alone, I tried contacting her again but she didn't took my call again, I asked megha to call her but she didn't pick her call also I left toward the canteen to look for her, when I reached the stairs I received a call from Apurva, she asked me where I am, I asked her to meet me at the ICT lab, I came down and waited for her at the ICT lab, she came and we exchanged greetings, she asked me where I was going, I told her that I am looking for Nidhi and I need to talk to her,

Dhruv was very much worried last night about her and his relationship,

"yeah I know, he called me last evening and it was evident in his voice that he was about to cry but was somehow managing to hold on, but yaar I didn't like him to be so much helpless and worried so I had asked him that I'll talk to Nidhi about this and try to sort this out, that's why I was also looking for her, I had even called her but she didn't answered my call, so I thought she might be with you, but you yourself are looking for her" said Apurva, she was also looking for Nidhi, I asked her to try calling her again, she might pick her call but all the attempts were in vain, so I asked her to come with me as I was going toward canteen to look for her.

# CHAPTER:- 12
# SHE BROKE UP

"Vipul I know yaar, neither of them is wrong in this but just a misunderstanding between the two, Dhruv should understand that he at any cost should get time for Nidhi and Nidhi should understand that her Dhruv will be back to her once he gets free from all this, but none of them is ready to understand the things, leave alone me if Nidhi would have told me that she has an issue with me, I would've separated out myself from his life, moreover she should not be insecure about me, he is just my friend like you, just he and I are like minded, just this makes me more attached to him, and that too just as a friend, neither he nor I have ever thought about each other more than this, but yaar its not ok that she is not understanding this" Apurva said while we were walking toward the canteen

"leave it yaar what has gone in the past, Dhruv is my best friend and my only good friend since the past 4 years and I can't see him like this, I want to clear this clutter anyhow. Nidhi has to understand and Dhruv should be back leaving all this, but all this should come to an end" I replied and we stepped in the canteen, I saw Nidhi sitting at the corner bench of the canteen looking out through the window, her bag was lying on one side, her phone was lying in front of her, I waited there and called on her phone to check if she is knowingly not picking the phone or she is not aware that I am calling her. Her phone rang, she saw it ringing picked the phone saw the screen and put it down, she was knowingly not picking my phone, I made Apurva call her for the last time, she saw her phone picked up her call this time,

"hey, where are you? I've been calling you for a while now," Apurva tried to look cool and calm in her voice

"why are you looking for me? Is Dhruv not with you?" Nidhi replied sarcastically, it hurt Apurva that she is not comfortable with her friendship with Dhruv, but she didn't show her feelings in her voice and replied

"no, he is out somewhere and I was in my class, just came out, thought to spend some time with you"

"oh! that's why you are looking for me, btw I am in canteen" Nidhi put another sarcasm in her sentence, Apurva ignored all the sharp tonts by Nidhi because she wanted to finish all this off and give Dhruv a new beginning as she was also concerned about Nidhi and Dhruv, Dhruv was her best friend and so she didn't wanted any kiosk in her life and she didn't wanted to hurt Nidhi as well because she considered her as a good friend, so she controlled herself and asked, "if you don't mind, can I come to you?"

"yeah sure, come I am here only" replied Nidhi,

"ok, just coming" Apurva replied and hung up the call, we waited there for a few minutes and then went to her,

Nidhi looked unhappy seeing me with Apurva and gave a very weird expression and picked her bag to keep it on the other side to give us space to sit, I took the stool in front of her,

"yaar, what I have done? Why aren't you picking my phone? Nidhi I just wanted to make Dhruv talk to you that time, because you didn't pick his call and he badly wanted to talk to you, you cut the call at that time and since then you are not picking my phone"

"if you've come to talk about that, I am in no mood to talk about those things which has become worse day by day and that person didn't even bother himself to spend a few moments with me, to atleast assure me he is still there with me, Vipul please you know each and everything about us since the very first day………," she didn't speak after that and her eyes filled with tears in them and her voice became heavy,

"excuse me please, I don't want to talk about it" she said and left from there.

We followed her but I stopped after a few steps to leave her with her space but Apurva followed her asked Nidhi to please let her talk, whatever be in Nidhi's mind but she never ignored or avoided talking to Apurva, so Apurva somehow convinced her to talk, and they both sat down in the ground near the guard room, I messaged Apurva to ask if I should come or not, she asked me not to come toward them as Nidhi might not like it and may not talk to her also, so I waited near the canteen only for Apurva to return, I knew Nidhi will not talk to me at this point of time, so she will not come with Apurva.

"Nidhi I know you are very disheartened by all this, I know Dhruv is wrong that he is not giving you proper time, I know he is wrong that he is not even meeting you in college, I know he is wrong that he is talking to everyone and not spending a minute with you, but Nidhi you should try to understand na that he is not in a situation currently that he could talk to you, he has even asked me not to remain and talk to him in college a few days ago, Nidhi he told you in the beginning itself about Sohail contesting the elections and you know very well if he commits to help someone he gives his 200% to that and you only asked him to help Sohail with all this and now just a few days more, he'll be back to you, like he was" Apurva tried to explain Nidhi

"Apurva don't drag yourself into all this, you go and take your classes, you have just entered your college life, you need to focus on your studies" answered Nidhi

"dude he is my friend and he was very anxious yesterday, he is not able to focus on anything, he wanted to talk to you, but you are not taking his calls since the last few days, dude I don't like him to be like this. Dude he tries to get some time to spend some time with you, but one or the person is always with him, he is always surrounded by some peoples, he don't wants to make people raise a brow on you, the other contender in front of Sohail always sends a person to be with Dhruv so that whatever he does is known to them, he has been taken by them a few times and was dropped somewhere so that he could not remain in college, just because of all this disturbances he tries to keep you away from all this, please try to understand his point too, I know you both love each other a lot and you both want to be together, but the situations are not that you this can happen at this time, Nidhi just like you are disheartened and hurt he is also not happy to remain away from you please talk to him on call for once and assure him that you are with him in all the situations, I am sure you both will feel relieved" Apurva said "you have nothing to do with it yaar, please don't waste your time on this, and moreover he is completely with you, he is spending time with you, he is talking to you, he is there with you in all your ups and down, how would you know about what I feel" Nidhi again put a sarcasm in her tone

"oh yeah, I was not coming to that as I had myself thought of keeping a distance with Dhruv because you don't like it, but if you want to talk about this, Nidhi if you would've told me that you don't like my friendship with him, I would never befriend him, and would've always kept a distance with her, but since the starting itself you always remained like, it doesn't bother you that I am his friend, he told me yesterday about this, and asked me to remain away from him as you don't like it, Nidhi I am just his friend and he is even ready to lose a friend for you and please don't worry from my side I'll not talk to him from now on" Apurva said in a high tone

"ok fine, I got your point and I'll see what I will do" Nidhi replied

Apurva requested her again to talk to Dhruv and left from there leaving Nidhi alone, it looked like Nidhi didn't liked Apurva talking to her about Dhruv and she became more tensed after this as if her disappointments had converted into anger. She remained sitting there deeply immersed in her thoughts till megha called her for the class as the professor had come to the class, she came and sat at the back bench so that no-one notices her.

"Vipul bhai, did you talked to her" Dhruv messaged me

"I tried talking to her but she didn't want to talk to me, Apurva talked to her for a while but it seems like she is more tensed since then" I replied

"dude where is she currently, I am coming to college and I want to talk to her" he asked

"we are in class and she is sitting alone on the corner bench" I replied

"Vipul, when will the class get over" he asked

"the class is till 1:30 but if it gets over before that, I'll text you" I told him

"koi ni I'll be waiting outside the class" he said

He came to the college and somehow managed to escape himself from everyone and told Sohail that he's going to talk to Nidhi, Sohail knew about the tension between them and somewhere he held himself responsible for this so he asked Dhruv that he'll also come in a few minutes,  Dhruv waited outside the class for the class to get over and as soon as the professor left the class he came in and went to Nidhi,

"Nidhi why are you doing like this? Why are you not picking up my call? why aren't you talking to me? Nidhi I am your Dhruv, I'll always be yours please try to understand yaar" Dhruv said

"Dhruv please leave me alone, I don't want to talk to you" Nidhi said furiously that everyone's eyes turned toward them, Dhruv felt like a culprit as is he is teasing a girl

"Nidhi talk to me na" he said

"go and talk to your Apurva, with whom you always talk to, with whom you spend all your time, who knows you more than me, who was telling me about you, a new friend is telling your girlfriend about you, how strange, Dhruv go yaar, I don't want to talk to her, go celebrate her birthday, bring a cake for her, enjoy your moments with her, and in the end when you'll not able to study properly for the exams, put the blame on me." She shouted all this and all the people around were listening to this

"Nidhi I promise I'll leave all this and spend all my time with you, I will always talk to you and will talk to you only, I won't talk to any other person, please forgive me for all this, I could not do anything these days, sorry yaar please forgive me" he cried

"Dhruv I don't want to create a scene" she said

"is anything left now, everyone heard all the things, there is nothing between us only" Dhruv said, hurt by the way Nidhi shouted on him

"look who is talking about keeping things between us, who tells each and everything to his friend, who has not kept even a single thing between us, Mr. Dhruv if I had a problem with that girl being with you, it was your responsibility to maintain a distance with her for me and even not tell her what I think of her you should've defended me and not told her that Nidhi has a problem with her. Nidhi's problem should've been yours and you should've sorted this out and made me feel comfortable and not just go and ask her to keep a distance because I don't like, not because you don't want to get close to her, it seems like you are enjoying her company but I am controlling you not to talk to anyone, Mr. Dhruv try to understand this is not what you should've done" Nidhi shouted on him

"you're getting me wrong yaar, it is not like that, I always wanted to spend time with you and always wanted to talk to you. I wanted to meet you but I couldn't yaar" he was saying all this when Sohail came, he saw Sohail and said "Sohail tell her na, how we have managed to escape today, how we spend the time in college and by what time do we get free in the evening"

"see Dhruv I don't want any explanation from anyone, it's just you and I who should be responsible for this, you didn't spend time with me, you didn't talked to me properly, you tried to control me, you asked me not to meet you, you were very much comfortable with that girl but when it comes to me you have many excuses about this and that, it's been a long time that we've been dragging this relationship, lets mutually come to an end and separate from each other, I don't feel like being with you anymore" Nidhi said

"Nidhi what are you saying yaar, we can sort this out, I'll do whatever you want me to do, I'll never talk to anyone, I'll never go away from you, please don't say this" Dhruv cried in front of her

"I don't want to control your life and I don't want to sort anything now, I don't want to spoil your studies like I did in 1$^{st}$ semester, I don't want you to separate you from your friends, I don't want you to do anything for me, just do me a favor and leave me now" Nidhi joined her hands and left

I could see tears in her eyes as well but she took a decision to break up with Dhruv and end the relationship which was about to be a year old in the next few day. Dhruv remained sitting there and Nidhi left and she was also not happy and was very much broke by this, I tried talking to her but she also broke and went into the washroom.

Apurva came from behind and asked me about what happened, I told her everything and she ran toward Dhruv.

All the memories, love, affection, attraction, and all the feelings they had for each other came to an end. Dhruv kept sitting there, Apurva, Sohail and I sat near him and tried to control him but he was uncontrollable and kept on crying and wiping his tears. Nidhi went in the girl's common room and she was also not talking to anyone and just sitting alone with herself trying to digest all that had happened just now.

# CHAPTER:- 13
# THE LAST DIARY ENTRY

The days and months passed by but the life of Nidhi and Dhruv didn't changed a bit. Nidhi remained alone and didn't talked to anyone, she just came to college, attended her classes and left. she didn't even talk much to megha and muskan. Dhruv completed his commitment and stopped coming to college after that, he studied at home, took notes from me and tried to limit himself into his home only, he also left all contacts with everyone, Apurva was the one who listened to his harsh words and faced his anger but never left his side, she always listened to him and tried to comfort him. Dhruv tried to break contact with her also, he shouted on her and even blamed her for everything that had happened in his life, but Apurva never left him and understood that Dhruv is disturbed and he is saying all this out of anger but deep inside he wanted a support and Apurva became that support for him in his harsh time.

Dhruv tried connecting to Nidhi a few times but Nidhi didn't talked to her anyhow, although she also wanted to talk to her but all that had happened in the last few days of their relationship restricted her from talking to him, she was also very much broke and hurt after separating from him but none can do anything and unite them until they themselves make a move toward each other but till now Nidhi was not able to forget about what had happened during that time and so she was not able to make a move, Nidhi also thought about the last day when they broke up from each other and recalled the scene in her mind and held herself responsible for what Dhruv might be facing at that time, she thought that she had spoken more than required out of anger and she should not have shouted on him, one reason behind why she was not able to talk to him was she was not able to grab enough courage to face Dhruv after all that she said.

By this time Nidhi had realized that she shouldn't have behaved in the manner that she did but it was too late for the realization because what she did created a wall between the two and the wall has become larger and larger since then, Dhruv also developed a feeling that Nidhi insulted him in front of everyone and all his feeling of love got overshadowed by this feeling of inferiority and hatred toward Nidhi for what she did.

But somewhere Dhruv always wanted to get his Nidhi back in his life, but this time his self-respect was not allowing him to make an initiative, ego was winning the battle between their love, one day while cleaning his room Dhruv found the diary which he used to write for Nidhi in that semester break when they were not talking, he decided to take that diary and start writing in it again, he left each and everything in his room as it is and sat on the table, he spend a few hours in reading what he had written earlier in that, somewhere he smiled while reading, somewhere he became a bit serious, somewhere his eyes became heavy and field with tears in them, somewhere he picked that diary and kept it on his heart, trying to feel Nidhi through that diary, he completed reading all the pages and took out the pens from his bag, those pens which Nidhi gifted him on his birthday, those sparkling ones which he had kept safe always and never used, he opened the diary from the backside this time and took a black pen and wrote a quote there,

*"Akele to hum Pehle bhi the, vo meri zindagi me aakar mujhe tanha kar gye"*

He wrote this quote on the back side and turned the pages and reached where he had left, and started writing;

Sunday, 23rd September,2018

5:25pm

Dear diary,

 I am back to you, many things had happened during this time when I didn't talk to you, I am sorry that I even forgot you, but from now on I won't leave you ever. You know I was alone before my college life but I used to enjoy each and every moment with my friend and family but since Nidhi left me, I am lonely now. Yes, Nidhi broke up with me, I tried much to be with her but she didn't listen to me for once and took the decision by herself, in the starting itself we had promised each other that we had come together by mutual concern and will take the steps and decisions ahead by mutual concern, she also fulfilled her promise but the last decision of separating from me was taken by her only, and since the time she had gone from my life I had confined myself to the four walls of this room, I only step out when mom or dad have some work or I need to go college for some urgent work, otherwise I don't go to college even, I don't have that much courage to face my classmates, they believe I am the sole responsible person for this relationship to end, Nidhi had shouted on me and blamed me in front of everyone, those who were not there also got this information about the incident from their friends, they saw me crying and no one talks to me now.

Yeah I forgot to tell you about Apurva, I have a friend named Apurva, she had always been there with me in this time, she never blames me for anything that happened, she neither blames Nidhi for all this, she is a sweet girl, she says that the situations were not good during that time and soon everything will be sorted and I'll have my Nidhi back in my life, she even tries to comfort me by telling that no-one believes it was my fault rather everyone knows that I had done my best to save the relationship and have my Nidhi in my life, but I don't get enough confidence to face any of them and hence I remain here only.

It has been a long time that I had seen Nidhi, I don't have even a single pic in my phone with her, I realized that when I used to remain with her, we were so much busy creating memories that we didn't get any time to capture them, sometimes I feel like talking to her but I don't know what stops me from doing so.

I don't know what I feel what I think what I do, but one thing is very much clear that if I can get my Nidhi back in my life, I would do anything for it……"

He wrote this much in his diary that day and sat there thinking about Nidhi, thinking and thinking he didn't know when he fell asleep and started dreaming,

"He was sitting on the bench at the corner of the park with a flower in his hand, thinking about her. He was completely lost in her thoughts, when he noticed a girl in white top and a blue jean entering the park from the back entrance. He was not able to recognize the face as she was somehow far from him, she was looking here and there seeking for someone in the park when she noticed him and started moving toward him, as she was moving close to him, he slowly recognized her, it was she, her love of life, about whom he was thinking of, she came and sat beside her, took the flower from his hand and held his hands, and kept her head on his shoulder, he looked in her eyes and lost himself in the deep ocean, she slowly shifted toward him and sat in his lap, both of them could feel each other's breathe, they were completely lost in each other, he held her from her waist and hugged her tight, his heart was so heavy that tears rolled down his cheeks and fell on her shoulder she also wrapped her arms around him and hugged him back with the same intensity, they didn't wanted anything to come between them, they were so close to each other that their heartbeat could be felt by them and even the air could not make its way between them.."

Nishant Jha

# EPILOGUE

it was our farewell and we all wanted to enjoy that event but Dhruv was in no mood to come for that too but I wanted Dhruv and Nidhi to meet for once before the college ends because after this they may not get any chance to meet and talk, so I insisted Dhruv to come to college.

"Vipul, don't do like this dude, you know I will not come. And I don't like saying no to you again and again" said Dhruv

"then don't say no to me and just get ready fast I am coming in an hour to pick you up, I am coming on daddy's car, just get ready or else if I reach before that you have to get ready in the car only"

I somehow convinced Dhruv to come to college and I had asked muskan to somehow convince Nidhi to come and she also became successful in doing so.

We enjoyed the whole day and while leaving we were clicking pictures with each other in groups and in couples also, in a flow Nidhi and Dhruv captures themselves in a frame and became silent.

"this is our first and last picture together" said Dhruv

"hmmmm" Nidhi was not able to say anything

"how did you spend this time?" asked Dhruv

"just like you did" "how will I be without you?" replied Nidhi

Dhruv smiled and became silent, it was like they both needed just a start and everything will be fine,

"I still love you" said Dhruv in a heavy voice, his throat filled with feelings

"I love you too idiot" answered Nidhi and pulled Dhruv toward him and hugged her tight.

"please forgive me for all I did, I know you might be very angry on me, you never wanted to talk to me but I missed you and me being us each and every day that I passed without you, I know I shouldn't have shouted on you, I know I should've tried to manage the situation in a different way, I know I should've given a second thought to everything I spoke, but believe me I spoke everything in anger and I didn't meant anything, please forgive me for all that, I thought wrong about Apurva, but she took care of you like a mother, she always stayed there with you when I left you, I am guilty that I thought wrong about her, please forgive me for that" Nidhi spoke keeping her head on his shoulder and continuously crying

"my dearest I was never angry on you about anything, I don't think that you were wrong anywhere, so for what should I forgive you" Dhruv held her shoulder and wiped her tears from her face and asked her to smile and promised him to be with her forever and give her time always

"but you should ask Apurva if she forgave you or not, I can't say anything on her behalf" Dhruv teased her

"what should I do?" Nidhi asked

"you should gift her something" Dhruv said

"oh guruji, you both are together and happy, this is the biggest gift for me, and moreover I was never furious on you, so chillax and enjoy and you Dhruv stop teasing her, otherwise if she leaves there will be no farewell to reunite you both" came Apurva saying and started laughing

Everyone laughed on this and they left to celebrate the moment

* 9 7 9 8 6 6 8 4 2 5 3 3 4 *